I0797062

Tales from Ondiran:

The Eye of Ksera

Sorceress for Hire

Sinta, Sorceress-Detective

The Misadventures of Thonir

The Court Sorcerers
(expected, 2025)

SEDIGITUS SWIFT

Sorceress for Hire

Archelaus
Washington, DC

Published by *Archelaus*

archelaus-cards.com

Cover art by Glen Evans

ISBN 978-1-961852-03-7 (paperback)
ISBN 978-1-961852-02-0 (ebook)

Sorceress for Hire

Tales from Ondiran, Book Two

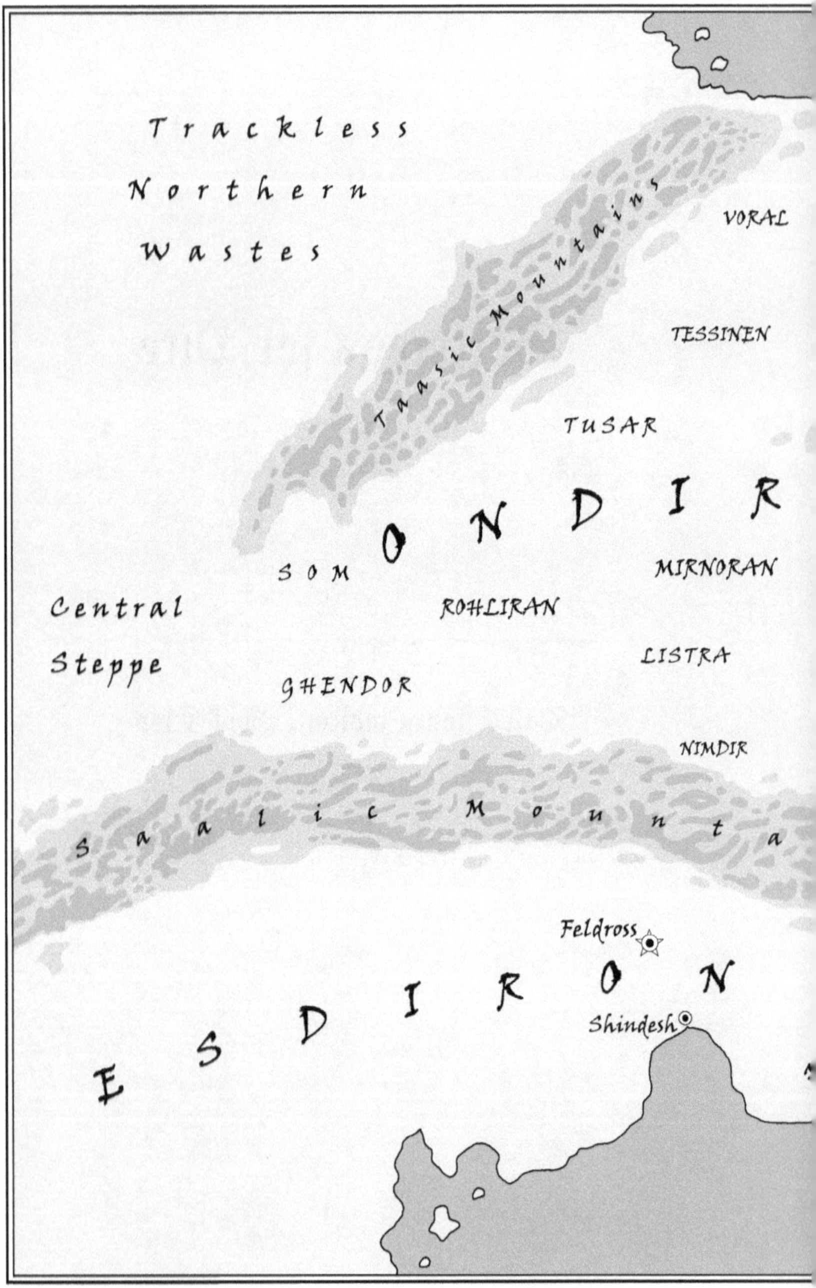

Trackless
Northern
Wastes

Taasic Mountains

VORAL

TESSINEN

TUSAR

ONDIR

SOM

MIRNORAN

Central
Steppe

ROHLIRAN

LISTRA

GHENDOR

NIMDIR

Saalic Mounta

Feldross

ESDIRON

Shindesh

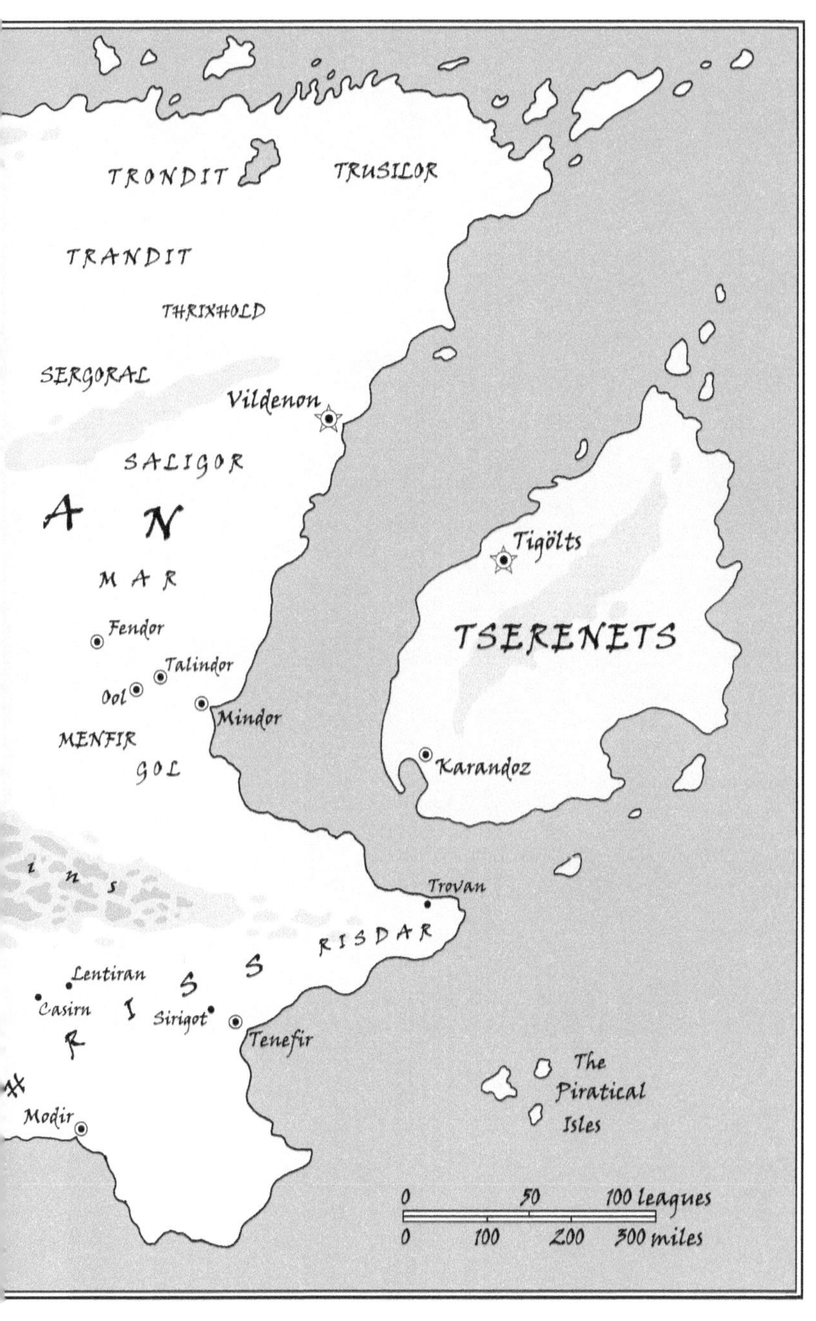

TRONDIT
TRUSILOR
TRANDIT
THRIXHOLD
SERGORAL
Vildenon
SALIGOR
A N
MAR
Tigölts
TSERENETS
Fendor
Talindor
Ool
Mindor
MENFIR
GOL
Karandoz
i n s
Trovan
RISDAR
S
Lentiran
S
Casirn
I
Sirigot
Tenefir
R
Modir
The
Piratical
Isles
0
50
100 leagues
0
100
200
300 miles

1

The Duchy of Hriss, the southernmost province of Ondiran, has maintained a distinctive cultural identity within the Empire since early medieval times. Unfortunately, sharing a border with Esdiron has had a deleterious effect upon the duchy. The Hrissic dialect deviates markedly from the Ondiric literary standard. The religious life of the duchy, too, has been polluted by several cults of Esdiric origin. Hriss is a fertile province, however, with a milder climate than the rest of Ondiran, permitting the cultivation of a wider variety of crops. Its wines are particularly noteworthy. Tenefir, the ducal seat, is a major port that has long been a center of Ondiric trade with both Esdiron and Iniroch, not to speak of the exotic lands farther to the west.

— *The Phantom Empire: A Historical Geography of Ondiran*

"You want me to find a lost dog?" Sinta was unable to keep the incredulity out of her voice. Was she not a highly skilled sorceress? Had she not studied under one of the foremost magical minds in all Ondiran? Had she really been reduced to competing for business with Sog, Tenefir's dim-witted municipal dog- and rat-catcher, whose duties included removing horse manure from the city streets?

Her prospective client, a fashionably plump and pampered baroness, frowned. "I'm not sure I like your tone. My sweet little Faika is a treasured member of this family, this *noble* family, and I want her found!"

Sinta swallowed her annoyance along with her pride. "Yes, of course, milady." She had a living to make (and in all fairness, if her pet lizard, Angvar, went missing, she would certainly want him found). With a sigh, she elicited a full description of the dog, inquired after its particular habits, and established when it had last been seen. Since the animal appeared to have been fully as plump and pampered as its mistress, dividing the bulk of its time between the baroness's lap and a plush cushion in the baroness's bedchamber, Sinta concluded that it was more likely to have been stolen than to have strayed. Accordingly, she requested leave to interview the servants in private.

Rilde, lady's maid to the baroness, came first, as she had the most contact with the creature. Her protestations of abiding love for "dear Faika" rang false, particularly in view of several imperfectly healed bites on her hands and wrists, so Sinta cast a discreet charm spell and invited her to explain how she really felt about the dog.

"Nasty little beast," Rilde confided. "Gets the choicest treats from the table, and all it does in return is sleep, crap, and pee. Oh, and snap at anyone who isn't the mistress. It does that, too."

Sinta asked about Faika's mysterious disappearance.

"Popped the little monster into a basket, didn't I," replied Rilde. "Gave it to Rosso (that's our second footman), and he took it out and sold it to some western sailors down at the docks. They eat dogs, you know, those crazy westerners!"

After recovering Rilde's share of the modest take, Sinta summoned Rosso, a good-looking young man from the island kingdom of Tserenets. (She had noticed that footmen, like chambermaids, were expected to be decorative.) Sinta spoke Tseren well, so she chose to conduct the interview in that language as a confidence-building measure. Confronted with Rilde's confession, Rosso quickly folded—without recourse to magic on Sinta's part—and did his best to describe the sailors' ship for her. After prevailing upon him to turn over his share of the money, Sinta hastened down to the docks, hoping—more for the sake of her fee than from any particular feeling of benevolence toward the missing canine—that she would not be too late.

The docks reeked of brine and dead fish, as the raucous cries of a thousand squabbling gulls rent the air. Sinta quickly found several merchant vessels with female figureheads, as described by Rosso, but only one of obviously western design, with a western crew, and a name in western characters that she could not read. Learning a western language remained on the young sorceress's to-do list. Luckily, the boatswain, whom she found supervising maintenance of the ship's rigging, spoke enough Ondiric for them to communicate.

The first order of business was disabusing him of the assumption that she must be a prostitute. Respectable young women seldom came down to the docks and accosted sailors, so it was a natural—if tiresome—misconception. Sinta sighed. No, the pretty miss did not want to come aboard and earn some easy money. She was here for another reason entirely. Had a man sold them a dog yesterday, a small dog with silver fur? He had? Did they still have said dog? They did? Excellent. Yes, she knew dogs made good eating. But had they eaten this particular dog yet? They hadn't? Well, had they butchered—that is to say, had they killed—it yet? No? Very good. She was here to buy the animal back. She exhibited her coin purse and gave the contents a jingle.

The ship's first mate had to be summoned from below decks for the negotiation that followed, as he was the one who had made the original purchase. His Ondiric may have been better than the boatswain's, but he was no less eager to persuade Sinta to come aboard, arguing that if she really wanted this dog, they could easily reach a mutually advantageous barter agreement in his cabin. Sinta, however, declined to leave the safety of the wharf and insisted upon a purely cash transaction. Disappointed, the first mate demanded double what he had paid for the creature. Sinta, who had long experience bargaining at market, scoffed and offered one quarter. The first mate clutched his ears in an interesting western expression of scandalized disbelief that Sinta had not seen before. He then made an indignant remark in his own language, prompting the other sailors to stamp their feet and begin a fierce ululation that Sinta found unnerving. Feeling a need to rebalance the negotiation, she waved one hand above her head, releasing a shower of sizzling multicolored sparks that rose some fifteen feet in the air. The sailors' ululation came to an abrupt halt. The first mate lowered his price slightly, and Sinta raised her offer by a correspondingly meager amount, after which the haggling continued for another quarter of an hour, without further interruptions, until the two finally settled on what both of them knew to be fair from the beginning, namely the original purchase price.

Having completed the transaction to her satisfaction, Sinta peered into the now soiled and smelly basket at the snarling ball of silver fur inside. “If it weren’t for me,” she informed Faika, “they’d soon be serving you up, perhaps in a nice garlic sauce, garnished with fresh herbs.” The dog showed no sign of being impressed, let alone grateful, and continued to display its sharp little teeth. Sinta set down the basket, recalled to mind a spell to charm animals that she had learned early in her apprenticeship, and cast it. “Do not bite,” she then commanded. “Not me and not Rilde. Much though it may pain you, you must now be a good dog.”

Faika stopped snarling and whined petulantly instead.

“I’m glad we understand one another,” Sinta said, adding irrelevantly, “also, that you’re not a fish or an arthropod.” She released the creature from its filthy basket, which she then discarded upon a nearby pile of maritime rubbish. “Now, follow me!”

Faika meekly obeyed, trailing behind Sinta, back to the baroness’s ostentatious townhouse, where a tearful reunion ensued. When the baroness nevertheless quibbled about Sinta’s fee, the sorceress felt compelled to hint that she might turn Faika into a melon if the sum previously agreed upon were not forthcoming. While she did not actually know such a spell, she judged correctly that the baroness would not call her bluff. Annoyed at the attempt to cheat her, Sinta then yielded to an uncharacteristically malicious impulse. "I should warn you that I found Faika cavorting with a hideous spotted mongrel," she alleged to the baroness's horror, "so there may well be a litter of pups in a couple of months."

"Just be glad I didn't tell her the true story," Sinta told Rilde as she prepared to leave. "You will find Faika more manageable now, though I can't be sure how long my spell will last. I put a lot of power into it, but it's also very contrary to that animal's nature, so she will do her best to fight it. Still, when the spell does wear off, you can always bring her to me, and I'll be happy to refresh it for a modest sum."

2

Although the ancient philosopher Tirresofis made several significant contributions to the study of geometry, he and his followers are now primarily remembered for their eccentricities. They refused, for example, to eat goat meat, bathe in river water, or pay taxes. Tirresofis was executed by drowning at the age of seventy-four after he declined to pay the royal impost on imported figs.

—*Mathematicians of the Ancient World: A Guide for Young People*

Sinta sighed and fed Angvar a grub. A week had gone by with no new commissions, and she was feeling discouraged about her prospects as a freelance sorceress. Barely twenty, she found that potential clients tended to hold both her age and her sex against her. Young magicians often did security work of various kinds (for there was always a demand for enchantments to protect houses and shops from intruders, and traveling merchants generally felt safer with a spell caster along), but the prevailing view was that this sort of thing was better handled by men. Admittedly, Sinta herself was not particularly eager to accept assignments that might require her to slaughter entire bandit gangs or sink pirate ships with the loss of all hands. Her interest in magic was intellectual, not homicidal.

To be sure, when it came to the market for love philters, there was, if anything, a bias in favor of the work of female spell casters, but Sinta felt ethically constrained to turn away the heartsick men and women who sometimes came to her, desperate to overcome the perplexing indifference of those with whom they were besotted. She knew there was good money to be made in that line of magic, but however much she may have sympathized with the lovelorn, she also felt she had to respect the honest—and, in some cases, no doubt astute—preferences of those who rejected them.

Adding to her woes, Sinta had a well-established local competitor, a young wizard who had the advantage of being the son of an influential member of the Tenefir Merchant Guild, a connection he exploited for all it was worth. Sinta knew that he resented her intrusion into his territory, all the more so since—in addition to her strong background as a sorceress—she knew nearly as many wizarding spells as he did.

A tap on the door interrupted Sinta's melancholy reflections. Her landlady, Madam Imurga, entered. "Young man to see you," she announced. "Good-looking lad," she added, as though this information were somehow pertinent. A widow in her early sixties, Imurga had, so far as Sinta could determine, three consuming interests: her five house-rabbits, the writings of the ancient philosopher Tirresofis, and her tenant's love life. The rabbits, all gelded bucks, Sinta found agreeable enough. The philosophy she would have found interesting, had she trusted Imurga's commentary. The eagerness to find her a husband, she found tiresome in the extreme. There would be time enough for such things later, she felt. For the present, she had other priorities.

"Thank you, Imurga. Please tell him I will be down directly." She took a moment to tidy her appearance, in the hope of looking like a competent professional, and placed Angvar on her shoulder, in the belief that the crested green lizard gave her a certain presence. Doing her best to display good posture, notwithstanding the weight of the eighteen-inch reptile, she descended the stairs.

Imurga had not exaggerated. Sinta's caller, a tall, broad-shouldered, dark-haired man of about her own age, would have made an admirable footman, though he was more expensively attired. He bowed gracefully. "I am Othir, son of Osendir of Crin and presently squire to Pirendor, the Sixth Baron of Sirigot. My lord and master bids you greetings—as indeed I hasten to do myself."

Sinta did her best to curtsy without losing her balance or tumbling Angvar onto Madam Imurga's worn but still decorative carpet.

Othir presented her with a letter bearing an elaborate seal in red wax. "The baron is given to understand that you possess not only the arcane knowledge but also the capacity and skill to enchant armor. He is understandably anxious to secure your services."

Pleased to hear it, Sinta broke the seal and looked over the letter. Enchanted armor was in vanishingly short supply—as were those few magicians who knew the secrets of its manufacture—while the demand for it was great. Though Ondiric economic thinkers had yet to articulate a coherent theory of market equilibrium, the simplest peasant woman could have told them that under such circumstances enchanting armor would be a lucrative proposition. Sinta had done it only once before, but the proceeds were the chief reason she was still living at Madam Imurga's and not sheltering under a bridge somewhere.

"The baron writes of his wish to have a hauberk newly made," she noted. "That is good. While I can enchant existing armor, the results will be far better if I can work with the armorer from the beginning."

Othir inclined his head slightly in acknowledgement. "The armorer has in fact been directed to await your arrival. Assuming you are interested, I have instructions to escort you to Sirigot to discuss terms with his lordship—perhaps this very afternoon?" Seeing Sinta nod, he smiled. "Excellent! In the meantime, perhaps I could convince *you* to escort *me* somewhere nearby for a wholesome noon-time meal at my lord and master's expense. The ride from Sirigot has given me a healthy appetite."

❦

Having subsisted for some weeks chiefly on bread and cheese, Sinta enjoyed the roast pork with dumplings, though she declined the wine. She had never developed a taste for it and preferred to keep a clear head in the company of a stranger, even if he was well-born and charming (or perhaps especially then). She listened as he spoke entertainingly about life as a squire and his soon-to-be-completed training as a knight. He made it sound a good deal more amusing and less brutal than she suspected it was in reality.

For his part, Othir was observing Sinta more closely than she would have guessed from his flippant manner and self-centered conversation. He had expected the sorceress to be older and more physically imposing (for Sinta was in fact rather petite), with perhaps a more glamorous taste in clothes. He nevertheless sensed the lively intelligence behind her eyes and respected the caution with which she sat quietly appraising him. He was fully aware of the effect his looks often had on women, and though his own erotic preferences lay in the opposite direction, he could appreciate someone of either sex who had no intention of taking him at face value.

After lunch he patiently endured a discourse from Madam Imurga on Tirresofis's idiosyncratic views regarding the bisection of oblique angles, while Sinta hastily packed for the trip to Sirigot, pulling together a change of clothes, her notes on enchanting armor, and of course her trusty quarterstaff for self-defense. Afterward, the two went to a nearby livery stable, where Othir's horse, a spirited gray courser, greeted him with an affectionate nuzzle. The young man had trained the animal himself, eschewing the brutal methods commonly recommended, and he was proud of the results. For her part, Sinta had an arrangement with the stable, permitting her to rent a mount for short periods by purchasing a horse on the understanding that she could sell the animal back at a predetermined discount upon her return. She accordingly picked out a quiet chestnut rouncey within her price range. Nervous around horses, she always cast her animal charm on them before approaching too close. "You and I are going to be friends," she informed this one firmly. "And don't you forget it!"

⸙

The early spring weather had turned chilly. Wishing she had worn a warmer cloak, Sinta quietly cast a quick warming spell on herself as they rode. A mere three weeks had passed since the vernal equinox, when the Ondiric Civic Calendar had entered its seventy-first year. This well-conceived solar calendar had been a rare success for the usually feckless imperial authorities, providing as it did some much-needed uniformity in a land regulated by four or five major religious calendars, plus a slew of minor ones, most of them lunar (which, in a world with two moons, could result in eccentric timekeeping).

The road from Tenefir to Sirigot passed through some of the most productive agricultural land in the duchy. Not having lived in Hriss for long, Sinta observed with interest the differences between it and the countryside to which she was more accustomed. Newly sown fields near Tenefir increasingly gave way to established vineyards and orchards as they approached Sirigot. Rows of elongated peasant houses, windowless with narrow frontages, formed the occasional featureless village, built without even a central square.

As they rode, Othir stopped talking about himself—a topic, Sinta had to admit, concerning which he could be quite amusing—and began to ask questions about *her*. As a result, Sinta found herself telling him about her adventures as an apprentice to the powerful sorceress Lady Valdira of Fendoran, as well as the difficulties of making a name for herself as a freelance practitioner. "There is no magicians' guild to regulate these matters," she explained, "but most novice sorcerers and wizards—unless they have private means—enter into what amounts to a journeyman phase, taking commissions here and there from men like your Lord Pirendor, in the hope that a permanent position eventually presents itself. It's a question of relying upon word-of-mouth to develop a reputation for quality work and discretion over time."

Othir smiled. "Well, you seem to be doing that, all right. My lord and master's cousin, Doromir of Tross, couldn't stop talking about the chainmail you enchanted for him. He said it was like wearing an impenetrable coat of liquid iron—though presumably without the searing heat and horrific burns."

Sinta laughed. "Let's just hope Lord Pirendor is likewise impressed."

Sinta's reference to sorcerers and wizards prompted Othir to ask about the difference between them. Both sorcery and wizardry were practiced in the Duchy of Hriss, without—so far as he could tell—a great deal to distinguish them. Sinta explained that the two systems of magic were built upon different mystical languages. "You find sorcerers mostly in Ondiran and Tserenets, and wizards mostly in Esdiron and Iniroch, with Hriss as neutral ground between them, but the fact is that the two systems are built upon similar underlying principles. A sorcerer who takes the trouble to learn the wizarding language doesn't have much difficulty casting wizarding spells and vice versa. Naturally, some spells are found only in one system or the other, and a few are better implemented in one than in the other, but there's really much more overlap than the partisans on either side are inclined to admit."

Othir snorted. "Well, if it's in part an Esdir-Ondir thing, I'm not surprised." The Esdir and the Ondir traditionally regarded one another with ill-disguised contempt.

As they neared Sirigot, the riders came to a village in which a cadaverous man of indeterminate age stood atop a wagon, surrounded by a knot of credulous peasants. He was holding up a small reliquary cheaply fashioned from tin. "I have here a *gen-u-ine* finger bone from the beloved Cantiferian saint, the holy Lady Brinna of Trinigot," he declared. "Her left second metacarpal," he added for the benefit of any budding anatomy students in the audience. "As you surely know, the venerable Brinna of sacred memory is the patron saint of all those who suffer from diseases uniquely afflicting womenfolk. Wear her relic around your neck, and you will be protected. If you already suffer, you will be cured." He set down the reliquary and picked up a glass vial of bright orange liquid. "And here is a magic potion to cure catarrh. Guaranteed effective!" He set it down. "But I wouldn't ask you to buy that. No, the good Dr. Hinnogrubir wouldn't ask you to part with your hard-earned money, even for a guaranteed cure. And why not? *Because he has something even better!*" He held up a stoppered ceramic flask. "This crucial concoction, this pluperfect panacea, this marvelous medicament—my own prize recipe—combining extracts of twelve curative herbs, three exotic health-giving spices, and one secret magical super-ingredient, all in a tincture of the purest alcohol, won't just cure catarrh! It won't just cure diseases of the heart and lungs, or of the stomach and bowels, or of the blood and bile, or of the bones and teeth! It won't just cure ailments of the skin, hair, and fingernails! Or lameness brought on by Hrodgir's Disease or blindness brought on by the Dandelion Blight! It will cure fever and ague! It will cure convulsions! It will cure dropsy and edema! It will cure necrosis! It will cure diarrhea, constipation, piles, and melancholy! It will cure masculine inadequacy and feminine frigidity!" The huckster paused for breath. "By god, what won't it cure?" he concluded rhetorically.

"Anything at all?" suggested Othir loudly.

The cadaverous man spun around to face him. "My friends, I see we have gentlefolk among us. Skeptical gentlefolk. My dear sir, purchase a flask for just one silver griffin, and I promise it will cure your skepticism!"

Sinta completed a spell and touched the side of her nose. "What's really in it?" she called out. "Tell the truth, now!"

The charlatan struggled visibly against the charm before succumbing to its power. "The gentle lady asks what's in it," he repeated, a pained expression on his face. "And such is my supreme confidence in the wondrous power of this elixir that I am not afraid to tell you, it consists chiefly of wood alcohol, with a splash of sheep's piss for flavoring."

This revelation provoked some indignant murmuring among the assembled peasants, though one or two still seemed interested in giving the wonder product a try. Nevertheless, the discomfited salesman hastened to depart before the angry rumblings could turn to violence. "Good day, good people," he called out, as he urged his horses into a trot, pulling his wagon away from the crowd. "Must dash. But never fear—I shall return!"

One or two of the peasants threw stones after him, but these bounced harmlessly off the back of the wagon.

Othir hooted with laughter. "Sheep's piss!" he repeated with delight.

Sinta frowned. "My father is an apothecary," she said. "An *honest* apothecary. I have no time for mountebanks who bring the profession into disrepute."

Othir brought his mirth under control. "Well, you saw *that one* off, anyway," he affirmed, "sheep's piss and all!"

3

Apart from a few poorly preserved medieval monuments, the town of Sirigot holds little of interest. We suggest skipping it in favor of the nearby university town of Tingoss with its youth culture and swinging nightlife.

—*Hriss on 10 Crowns a Day*

Sinta was relieved that Othir's liege lord, Pirendor, Sixth Baron of Sirigot—a heavy-set, fierce-looking man with a bristling red beard—quickly accepted her terms and contracted to pay the fee she demanded. Converted from the Fendoric currency in which she continued to think (having spent her apprenticeship in Fendoran), it amounted to a total of 360 Hrissic gold pendragons in three equal installments, corresponding to the three separate visits to Sirigot the sorceress would have to make over the coming months, as she worked with the local armorer during different phases of the hauberk's construction.

Sinta reflected—not for the first time—on the extraordinary complexity of monetary transactions in Ondiran, where every sovereign entity insisted upon minting its own coinage. Fortunately, the Duchy of Hriss boasted one of the most stable and widely accepted currencies on the Continent. Sinta was good at performing calculations in her head, but she still had difficulty coping with Hriss's eight different coins: 1 gold pendragon being worth 2 gold dragons, 3 gold wyverns, 24 silver griffins, 120 copper dragonets, 144 bronze falcons, 240 brass ferrets, or 960 tin starlings. Trying to remember the correct rate of exchange between the Hrissic ferret and the Fendoric penny, or between the Hrissic starling and the Fendoric farthing, was enough to drive her to distraction, though it was not nearly so bad as coping with all the other random Ondiric coins circulating in Hriss alongside the pendragon, not to mention the Esdiric *poog,* which had been badly debased by the current king of Esdiron, so that recent mintings contained up to a third less silver than older ones. Then, of course, there were underweight coins that had been clipped by dishonest members of the public, not to speak of outright counterfeits. One of the few coins Sinta had yet to encounter in daily use was the imperial crown, which was never minted in adequate quantities to serve its intended purpose of unifying the empire, though some merchant houses evidently found it useful as a unit of account. The whole situation was almost enough to make Sinta feel sorry for the professional moneychangers, who had to live and breathe this nonsense. Almost, but not quite.

At dinner, Sinta helped herself to extra servings of crispy roast goose and buttered parsnips. She did her best to make friendly conversation with the baron and his wife, but since small talk was not something she had studied as an apprentice, she was not very good at it. The baroness nevertheless condescended to declare her "charming" (quite without reference to her spell casting), so Sinta could hope she had not embarrassed herself too abjectly.

In the morning, she went with Othir to meet the master armorer, a short, muscular fellow named Virt, who was assisted by two journeymen and four apprentices. He seemed dubious, as Sinta explained the first stage of the process, which involved enchanting his tools and raw materials. Consulting her notes (which she had previously enchanted to protect them from stray sparks), Sinta cast the requisite spells upon the forge, with its bellows and slack tub, to make it work more efficiently, and upon a dedicated supply of charcoal, to make it burn hotter. She then turned her attention to the shop's anvils, along with its various hammers, tongs, and chisels, as well as the pile of scrap iron from which the hauberk would be manufactured. "At this stage," she explained, "I'm enchanting the metal to be as soft and pliable as possible, so as to ease and speed your work. The spell will eventually wear off, and then I'll enchant the metal again to harden it as much as possible, without rendering it brittle."

Virt put Sinta's spells to the test by hammering out some thin iron rods. The job went quickly, and he admitted to being impressed, remarking that it was almost like working with copper.

Chainmail is made from iron wire of a heavy gauge, wrought into interlocking rings. Sinta therefore next enchanted Virt's wire-drawing bench, a sturdy wooden contraption some six feet long with a windlass at one end that was used to squeeze the iron rods through a series of ever smaller holes in the draw plate at the other end, until they were finally stretched into wire of the diameter required. "This is where you will really see the benefit of the more pliable iron," she said. "You'll be needing, what, something over a mile of wire? Speeding up its production is a big advantage."

Virt drew a rod into wire of the correct gauge. "You apprentices should fall on your knees and kiss this woman's feet," he declared. "She's just vastly improved *your* lives over the next few weeks, I can tell you."

Relieved that none of the apprentices took this injunction literally, Sinta moved on to three jigs Virt had set up. Each had a dowel-like mandrel, around which the wire could be coiled like a spring, creating, when cut, the iron rings used to make the mail. Sinta also enchanted several sets of cutters, nippers, pliers, and gloves.

Virt took his length of enchanted wire, coiled it tight around one of the mandrels, removed the resulting spring, and then snipped his way through it to produce forty slightly overlapping iron rings. "I think that took about half the time it would have otherwise," he exulted. "As long as we don't end up with a suit of armor that's as soft as butter, I'm happy."

They placed the rings in the forge to anneal. "At this point," Sinta said, "we've reached the enchantments I'll be performing on my second visit with regard to the armor itself, but let's continue with the demonstration, so I can enchant the rest of the tools you'll be using." While they waited for the rings to cool, she cast spells on a variety of hammers, tongs, punches, and drifts.

Virt then began the intricate process of preparing each ring to be riveted shut, by flattening the overlap and punching a hole through both layers to take the rivets. He continued by snipping off tiny pieces of left-over wire to serve as the rivets themselves. Once again he professed himself pleased with the effects of Sinta's enchantment, as he pieced together the rings into a mesh—with each ring surrounded by four others—fastening the rivets with a special pliers as he went.

Her own work for the day completed, Sinta gratefully took the opportunity to sit down on a nearby bench. Casting so many spells in rapid succession, some of them very powerful magicks indeed, was physically exhausting. It also diminished her ability to cast further spells, which relied upon her innate magical power, or *korethi,* as it was known in the mystical language of sorcery. Each spell drained some away, and she would need rest—in particular a good night's sleep—to replenish it. Fortunately, she had succeeded in getting through all the spells she had intended to cast that morning without reaching the limit of her capacity, but she had cut it close.

Virt's wife announced lunch. If she was inclined to be a bit suspicious of the young and not unattractive sorceress who had arrived to work with her husband, she was flattered by the unladylike verve with which Sinta tucked into her rustic vegetable stew and blood sausage, and she was entirely won over by Sinta's promise to cast certain practical household spells on her next visit, including one that caused chamber pots to empty and clean themselves.

After lunch, Othir showed Sinta around Sirigot. It was, he admitted, an undistinguished town, but the ever inquisitive sorceress found it interesting all the same, for Esdiric cultural influences were noticeable, manifesting themselves in various ways, from vernacular architecture to the foods sold by street vendors. Othir proved a good guide in this respect, for he did not share the widespread Ondiric prejudice against the Esdir and could provide a sensible commentary on what they saw.

Unfortunately, Sinta was often prey to bad dreams when her *korethi* was low, particularly following a large meal. Although the day had been a success, that night she dreamt she was being watched by three wolves—one brown, one tawny, and one gray. All of them insisted on staring at her malevolently. She kept expecting them to speak, and when none chose to do so, she tried to tell them that she did not fear large, ravenous, slavering beasts, but no words came. Sinta did not believe in prophetic dreams, but she awoke the next morning feeling unsettled all the same.

4

To judge by surviving administrative records, what we would today call home invasion was a recurring problem even in the safer parts of medieval Ondiran. In the Duchy of Hriss, for example, no fewer than seven gangs of robbers were brought to justice during the thirty-year reign of Duke Borthir III for setting upon outlying farms and mills and terrorizing their inhabitants.

—*Crime and Punishment in Medieval Ondiran*

After breakfast, Sinta and Othir returned to the armorer's forge, where the apprentices were busy hammering out iron rods and drawing them into wire. Although Sinta had completed all the necessary spells the morning before, she had deliberately conserved her *korethi* by putting less power than needed into her enchantment of the charcoal and scrap iron. If she did not refresh those spells with much greater power today, they would lapse long before Virt could complete his work with them. She had explained all this to him the day before, so the armorer was expecting her.

"As you can see," he said, "my boys have been hard at work since yesterday afternoon. They've already drawn at least two normal days' worth of wire. So, cast your remaining spells, and we'll let you know when we're ready for you to come back."

Causing such a large quantity of charcoal and scrap iron to stay enchanted for weeks once again came close to depleting Sinta's *korethi,* and she was happy to sit quietly on a stump afterward and watch the apprentices work, while awaiting the lunch to which Virt's wife had been kind enough to invite her. Othir, who had other business to attend to, returned after midday to escort her back to Lord Pirendor's castle, where the baron unstintingly counted out 120 gold pendragons. Sinta stashed them in a special coin purse she had enchanted during her final year as an apprentice. To all appearances it was an ordinary purse inside and out, and usable as such, but the magic words *monstrous lizard,* spoken in the language of sorcery, opened it instead onto an extradimensional space that could hold up to a thousand coins, without any change in weight or bulk.

"Unfortunately, I can accompany you only as far as the crossroads at Fronith today," Othir told her as they made ready to set out. "That's less than an hour from Tenefir. Will you be all right riding the rest of the way by yourself? If not, we could easily postpone the trip until tomorrow."

Sinta felt a pang of anxiety at the idea of traveling alone, but she brushed it aside in an effort to emulate the fearlessness her mentor in magical studies, Lady Valdira, invariably displayed. After all, she told herself, the Duchy of Hriss was relatively safe. Unlike some parts of the world in which she had traveled, banditry was all but unknown there. "No, thank you. I'd rather get home today. If we leave now, I should arrive long before dark."

About forty minutes after Sinta and Othir had parted company at Fronith, the road passed a large, prosperous-looking mill alongside the River Tene. Realizing that her mount must be thirsty, Sinta diverted the rouncey onto the short path into the mill yard, where she knew there would be water. A more experienced person would have recognized that an open gate into an empty yard signaled something amiss, but Sinta did not notice.

The yard was of substantial size, with sturdy wooden buildings on both left and right. In the middle, an old worn-out millstone had been laid out flat and made into a low platform. At the far end of the yard stood the two-story stone millhouse, together with a solid half-timbered dwelling for the miller. Both structures were built on an artificial island formed by the channel that brought water from the river to the mill's giant wheel. At present, however, the sluice was closed and the wheel stood motionless. A wooden bridge strong enough to bear a heavily laden wagon spanned the channel, which was a good five feet wide.

The water level in the closed channel was too low for the rouncey to reach. Spying an old bucket next to the bridge, Sinta dismounted to retrieve it. No sooner had she reached the bridge, however, than the door of the building on the left side of the yard opened and a rough-looking man carrying a sack stepped out. At almost the same moment, a man of even rougher appearance emerged from the building on the right, leading a reluctant draft horse by the bridle. The first man had a long knife at his belt, the second, an axe. Sinta had walked into a robbery in progress.

"Whoa!" exclaimed the first man. "Who's the pretty wench? Pity we already shot our wads doin' that dried-out old husk of a miller's wife."

"Speak fer yerself!" scoffed the second, who was not about to admit that he lacked the capacity for a second rape. "Besides, we kin always take her with us and have our fun later."

For a moment, Sinta froze, her body paralyzed with fear. Her mind, however, remained sharp. Over the course of her apprenticeship she had developed an unusual capacity for thinking clearly under stress. As the two robbers advanced upon her from opposite sides, she reminded herself that she was a sorceress, damn it. She might have largely depleted her *korethi* with the morning's arduous enchantments, but she was not without resources. Fighting down her fear, she turned to face the second robber, who was the nearer of the two. "Kick the bad man!" she ordered her horse, as he loomed into range. Still under the effect of Sinta's charm spell, the rouncey pinned back its ears and lashed out behind with an iron-shod hoof, striking the robber's right thigh. The man swore and lost his grip on the bridle of the draft horse. This powerful animal then reared and—taking revenge upon the robber for a deeply resented act of cruelty minutes earlier in the stable—gave him a vicious kick of its own that caught the man in the small of the back and knocked him flat on his face.

"Good work, both of you!" Sinta cried. "Keep it up!" The charm did not actually require her to vocalize her commands (animals did not understand the spoken words anyway), but she calculated that a girl with a preternaturally obedient horse was more intimidating than a girl with a merely ornery one. And if she could persuade the robbers she had control of both horses, so much the better.

The rouncey kicked the fallen robber in the face, as he struggled to regain his feet. He crashed back onto his hands and knees, spitting blood and broken teeth.

"Hey, Grulfar, you'd better get out here," shouted the first robber. "There's some crazy shit goin' down!"

Sinta turned and saw that the first robber had prudently altered his previous intercept course in favor of blocking the exit gate. She responded by leaving the vicinity of the bridge and calling the rouncey to join her on the left side of the yard. If more robbers were in prospect, Sinta wanted to take up a position from which any spell she might throw could hit all of them at once. The draft horse followed her and the rouncey. She patted the enormous creature cautiously on the neck. Having neither the time nor the *korethi* to charm the animal, she was grateful it seemed to have cast its lot in with her of its own accord.

The door of the miller's house opened, and four more robbers emerged, laden with valuables. "What's going on, Ulf?" demanded Grulfar, their obvious leader, a tall, lean, brown-haired man, who was markedly better dressed and groomed than the others.

"That mad bitch made the horses attack Tigron," shouted the first robber. "Kicked the crap out of him, they did!"

Sprawled awkwardly on the ground clutching his bloodied face, the second robber endorsed this account as best he could with a series of inchoate noises.

"You don't say?" Grulfar sounded amused rather than concerned. "That wasn't very friendly, now then was it? We prefer our womenfolk friendly." He drew his sword, and the three robbers with him followed suit, producing various lesser weapons. "But we take them as we find them, don't we, boys? Especially the pretty ones."

Grulfar's men laughed nastily, and Sinta felt a new wave of fear sweep over her, beginning in the pit of her stomach and spreading outward to her extremities. She took several deep breaths in an effort to stop herself from shaking. These physiological phenomena reminded her, however, of a lesson she had drawn from her adventures as an apprentice, namely that quite simple spells affecting basic functions of the human body could be every bit as disruptive to one's opponents as showier and more difficult magicks. For a sorceress whose *korethi* was dangerously low, it was a valuable insight.

She waited until Grulfar and the other robbers from the miller's house had crossed the bridge and joined their two fellows. Then she summoned all the power she could muster for a quick incantation to render them all temporarily blind.

Sudden loss of sight is terrifying. Some of the robbers screamed. Others swore. One flailed foolishly about with his bludgeon, accidentally dealing a glancing blow to the shoulder of the man in front of him, who then slashed back ineffectually with his knife. The last robber off the bridge tried to back away from this noisy chaos, only to topple into the half-empty channel with a yell and a muddy splash.

Grulfar, however, showed no ill effects from the spell and continued to advance on Sinta with his sword. "So, the little minx is a spell caster," he exclaimed. "Well, well, well, my dear, I'm going to enjoy getting to know *you* a little better!"

Sinta blanched. She had been counting on that spell to ensure her escape. Now, her *korethi* exhausted, she saw no choice but to retrieve her quarterstaff from the improvised sling with which she had attached it to the rouncey's saddle. It was a fine weapon—a full six feet of solid oak, smooth and perfectly balanced, its tips shod with burnished iron—and she was skilled in its use, having begun training at fourteen. Under the circumstances, just feeling it back in her hands was calming. Nevertheless, a quarterstaff is no match for a sword. She would have to win this bout swiftly, or be cut to pieces.

Grulfar laughed. "So, you've got a staff, little girl. I'll knock it into kindling for you, shall I, before I introduce you to mine?" He gestured toward his crotch, lest she miss the obvious double entendre.

Sinta felt her fear turn to anger. Nevertheless, she resisted the temptation to show off some fancy moves with the quarterstaff. Rather than try to intimidate Grulfar, she would encourage him to underestimate her. Pretending to fumble with the staff, she silently ordered the rouncey to circle around and flank the man. *Move in close enough to make him nervous—but keep clear of that sword!* She hoped she was not taxing the animal's powers of comprehension with such complex instructions, but she had charmed many horses since learning the spell, and in her experience they were reasonably intelligent. This one did not let her down. With an aggressive squeal, it pranced menacingly, while staying just out of Grulfar's reach. Sinta was pleased to see the draft horse offer moral support, as well, baring its teeth at the robber and angrily swishing its tail.

Showing signs of wariness for the first time, Grulfar nonetheless closed on Sinta, who stopped pretending not to know what she was doing and adopted a combat stance. He made a first tentative thrust to see how she would react. Sinta dodged it easily, as her training took over. Exploiting the momentum she had gained, she did a pirouette and took a swing at his head. With a grunt, Grulfar ducked just in time to avoid a cracked skull, giving Sinta the opportunity to leap backward and regain a distance from which her weapon's longer reach would give her the advantage. Then, with her opponent momentarily distracted by another fierce squeal from the rouncey, she used the end of the staff to deliver a punch to the chest that staggered him.

"Right," he shouted, "I'm done playing, you crazy bitch!" Brandishing his sword, he once again closed the distance between them, determined to bring the fight to a brutal close.

Sinta realized that the contest had reached its decisive phase. If she did not end it now, Grulfar would surely kill her. As he set up a savage backhand, she took a chance and gave the flexed elbow of his sword arm a brisk rap. While not a powerful blow, it struck the ulnar nerve, with dramatic effect. Grulfar gave an anguished cry, as intense pain shot up and down his arm and his fingers relinquished their grip on the sword, which flew over his left shoulder and clattered to the ground behind him. Sinta followed up with what she considered a well-deserved thrust to the groin. Then, as Grulfar doubled over, she thumped him heavily on the back of the head. He fell to the ground and lay motionless, badly concussed.

Short of breath and shaking, Sinta vomited. Feeling only slightly better, she surveyed the scene. Four of the robbers, anxious to remove themselves from danger, had felt their way across the mill yard until they reached the corner where the wooden wall of the stable met the stone wall of the yard itself. The robber who had fallen into the channel was still cowering in the mud, evidently having decided it was safer to remain there than to climb out.

Sinta frowned, unsure how much longer her blindness spell would last. She summoned her most commanding voice (which was, admittedly, not very). "Throw down those weapons—and your loot." In response to a silent command, the rouncey moved in their direction and made threatening noises. "Don't try the patience of my horses,"

Sinta warned. "They'd just as soon crack your skulls as look at you!"

There was a clatter as an axe, a bludgeon, and three knives of differing lengths hit the ground, along with sacks stuffed with coins, household goods, and the miller's family heirlooms.

Sinta crossed the yard and tapped the largest of the men briskly on the ankle with her staff. "Don't forget that knife in your boot!" She was trying to decide what to do next, when she heard a door open. Turning, she saw a seventh robber emerge from the millhouse. He was a mere boy of about fifteen, whose eyes widened as they took in the unexpected situation in the yard. He looked as though he wanted to run, but being on an island, he had nowhere to go, short of diving into the river. (As he did not know how to swim, the lad declined to avail himself of that option.) Sinta pointed her quarterstaff at him. "You, there! Come here, or you'll regret it soon enough." The boy reluctantly crossed the bridge. "Gather up those weapons," Sinta told him, "and pile them on that old millstone over there, along with that dagger on your belt. Get moving!"

Sinta had the rouncey guard the gate in case the boy tried to make a run for it. She then considered how best to confine the robbers. Though well built, none of the mill's structures seemed likely to hold them for long once the blindness spell wore off. She therefore turned her attention to a heavy trapdoor set in the ground alongside the wooden building on the left side of the yard. When the boy finished moving the weapons, she ordered him to open it, revealing a well-stocked root cellar—small, but big enough, she decided, to hold seven, albeit not in comfort. She had the boy line up the other robbers and march them down into the cellar, until only Grulfar remained, still unconscious, where he had fallen. "Drag him over here," she ordered. "Roll him over and empty his pockets." She had not forgotten Grulfar's immunity to her blindness spell. She confiscated a suspect amulet. "All right, now it's time for the two of you to join your friends."

Had Sinta's spell endured another two minutes, all would probably have been well, but instead the robbers in the cellar—suddenly finding themselves able to see again—made a desperate attempt to escape, forcing Sinta to do some quick and brutal work with her quarterstaff. Seeing what he thought was his chance to get away, the youngest robber dashed like a hare for the gate, only to encounter the rouncey, which had not forgotten Sinta's instructions. After suffering a kick to the shin, the boy limped away from the gate and tried to scale the wall instead. Unfortunately for him, the rouncey chose to interpret its mandate expansively. Leaving the gate, it followed him, took a mouthful of buttock firmly between its teeth, and pulled him down.

"You'd better get back over here," Sinta advised, having subdued the other robbers, "unless you want to see what that animal can *really* do."

Rubbing his traumatized buttock, the boy obeyed. With a moan, he dragged Grulfar into the cellar after him and pulled the trapdoor closed.

Sinta breathed a sigh of relief. Since the door had neither lock nor latch, she directed the rouncey to stand on it. She would have used the draft horse, but she doubted the door could bear the weight of an animal that stood at least eighteen hands high. After a moment's reflection, she remembered why she had come into the mill yard in the first place and fetched a bucketful of clean water from the river. "You are a fine horse," she told the rouncey, as it gratefully drank its fill. "I may just have to keep you."

5

Apprehended after murdering the master miller Fassgir and perpetrating lewdness upon his wife, the robbers Fren, Ulf, Tigron, Hrigot, Teseer, and Voss confessed under examination to these as well as other infamous crimes against persons and property under the direction of their leader, Grulfar of Tiff. Executioner Nof carried out the just sentence of death-by-hanging upon the first five, the like sentence upon the sixth being commuted by reason of his youth. Grulfar, as ringleader, was broken on the wheel.

— *Chronicle of the Ducal City of Tenefir*

Knowing she could not leave the rouncey standing on the trapdoor indefinitely, Sinta ventured inside the wooden building on the left side of the yard to look for something else to use. There she was pleased to find a number of barrels filled with something heavy. She rolled them outside and set them upright on the door. Confident the cellar's inmates could not escape, she crossed the yard and took a cautious look inside the stable, which was empty except for a wagon. She then ventured across the bridge. With considerable trepidation at what she might find, she entered the miller's house.

It was worse than she feared. Just inside the door lay a large dog with its skull caved in. Sinta recalled that one of the robbers had a bloody kerchief wrapped around his wrist, consistent with his having bandaged a dog bite, so evidently the beast did not go down without a fight. Peering into the main room, Sinta saw the miller, dead on the floor, his naked body showing signs of torture. Beside him, in a state of forcible dishabille, his disheveled wife sobbed inconsolably. All around lay bits of broken crockery and other household wares. The robbers apparently enjoyed breaking what they did not steal.

Sinta tried to decide what to do. She had no idea what to say to this distraught woman, settling at last for: "You're safe now. The robbers are locked in your root cellar. They can't get out." She then ventured into some of the other rooms, which were in a comparable state of disarray. She returned with a blanket, which she placed around the woman's shoulders. "We've got to go into town," she told her. "You need first aid, and someone's got to come out and arrest the robbers." The woman continued to weep. "Wait here," Sinta told her. "I'll be right back."

She went out and hitched the draft horse to the wagon. Then she brought out the miller's wife and helped her into the back, where the poor woman curled up into a fetal position. The sorceress climbed up onto the front and shook the reins. "Walk on," she called to the draft horse. She whistled to the rouncey. "You come, too, of course."

❦

Dusk was falling as they arrived at Tenefir's northwestern gate. Sinta was glad to recognize one of the guards, who had come to her once for some minor job or other.

"Hriftar, isn't it?" she asked. "A gang of seven robbers attacked the big mill beside the road, about half a league from here. They murdered the miller and raped his wife. I left them trapped in the root cellar, but someone needs to take them into custody before they get out."

Raising his eyebrows, Hriftar promised to report it to the watch master immediately.

Sinta thanked him and drove the wagon to her lodgings. After entrusting the miller's wife to Madam Imurga, she took the horses and wagon to the livery stable. "I've decided to keep the rouncey," she told the owner, "and I'll need to board both horses, and store the wagon, at least for the next few days." She paid in advance, picked up her quarterstaff, spell notes, and bundle of dirty clothes, and walked back to Madam Imurga's.

She found the two women sipping hot broth in the kitchen. Although the miller's wife had stopped crying, she still had a dazed expression on her face—along with extensive cuts and bruises.

"Her name is Ilte," whispered Imurga. "Otherwise I haven't gotten a word out of her."

Sinta was not the daughter of an apothecary for nothing. She went upstairs to her room and busied herself with her collection of medicaments. After a time, she came back down and began gently to apply a sweet-smelling salve to the cuts on Ilte's face. "This will ease the pain and reduce the risk of infection," she explained. She pointed to the defensive wounds on Ilte's arms. "We'll need to apply it to those, as well."

Ilte seemed to be regaining some sort of awareness and began to cooperate with Sinta's efforts on her behalf.

Sinta looked her in the eye. "I'm sure you have more wounds on your legs and privities" (the archaic word popped into her head as an anodyne alternative for coarser terms), "but I think you will find it less distressing to apply the salve to those yourself, don't you?"

Ilte nodded hesitantly and began quietly to cry again.

"There, there, dear," said Madam Imurga. "Have some more broth."

First, however, Sinta had to finish applying the salve to Ilte's arms. "Have you already gone through the Change?" she asked gently.

Ilte nodded. "Last year," she whispered.

Sinta gave her a reassuring smile, relieved that there was no need to administer the herbal contraceptive she had prepared. "Do you want privacy to apply the rest of the salve, or do you want me to stay with you?"

Ilte opted for her to stay. Sinta asked Madam Imurga to make up a bed for their guest, though it would be another half an hour before she was fully treated and ready for it.

❦

That night in her own bed, the exhausted sorceress dreamt about wolves again. This time, however, the brown one was missing, while the gray one appeared angry, repeatedly baring its teeth and snarling. Sinta tried to explain that she was a powerful sorceress who had no cause to fear such creatures, but her lips refused to form the words. At length she woke up in a cold sweat, alone in the dark.

❧

Two days later, Sinta and Ilte received a summons to report to Master Nof, the municipal executioner, to give witness statements. Sinta knew Nof slightly, for he sold herbal remedies as a sideline. He was willing to disclose that he had all seven robbers in custody and that the town council had ordered him to use whatever coercive measures he deemed necessary to extract confessions from them. Sinta herself answered his questions with scrupulous care, not wishing to omit any inculpatory details, such as Ulf's admission that he and Tigron had participated in raping the miller's wife. A town clerk made a protocol of the interrogation, which Sinta read through and signed. She warned Nof that Ilte remained in a fragile state, and secured his promise that he would question her gently.

With that, Sinta's role in the prosecution of the robbers was complete. She declined to attend their subsequent execution, as she found such gruesome public spectacles horrifying, but she was glad that the criminals would be punished, as well as prevented from perpetrating future crimes. The judicial authorities commuted the sentence of the youngest robber, in part because he was only fifteen and in part because they were not fully convinced he had participated in either the miller's murder or Ilte's rape. The boy was thus merely branded on the forehead—to warn all who met him that he had been convicted of robbery—and banished from the town.

❦

Some eighty leagues to the west, an elderly servant quaked as he made his way down the stairs to a dark subterranean chamber, where a man with a long gray beard and a flowing black robe was fiddling with an alembic over a tabletop fire that appeared to be burning without fuel. "My lord," the servant began, his voice scarcely above a whisper, "alas, I am grieved to report that the outcome of the proceeding—I hesitate to call it a trial—is not that which you so devoutly and justly hoped."

The robed man glared at him. "Speak up, you fool! Spit it out, or I shall punish you for trifling with me."

The servant cringed and wrung his hands. "Of course, my lord. As you should! Placards appeared in Tenefir three days ago, proclaiming that all seven defendants were adjudged guilty, my lord."

The robed man swore in a language the servant did not understand. "I should have intervened more forcefully," he muttered. "What more?" he demanded.

"The execution, my lord, has already taken place."

The robed man swore again, this time in Ondiric. He glowered at his trembling lackey. "And my dear nephew, Grulfar—did he receive the silken rope befitting his rank?"

Having now reached the point of maximum danger, the servant winced. "No, my lord. He was—he was broken on the wheel, my lord."

"What?" screamed the robed man. "How outrageous! How disgraceful! How humiliating!" He picked up the alembic with a pair of tongs and hurled it at the wall, where it shattered, splashing the servant with boiling liquid. "Get out of my sight, you scoundrel!"

The poor man did not need to be told twice. Frankly, he had been expecting worse than a few scalding burns.

"Vengeance shall be mine," vowed the robed man. "First, disgrace and ruin; only then, a painful death."

Sinta might not know it, but she had made a dangerous enemy.

6

Religious practice across the lands of Ondiran is extremely diverse. There are, arguably, four major rites found throughout the Empire—Asardianism, Cantiferianism, Hrintism, and Zoorism—but over the centuries dozens of other cults have proliferated, some of which have attained regional significance. Prior to its suppression, the so-called Order of Mystical Knowledge enjoyed a significant following among those who purported to possess magical powers.

—*The Encyclopædia Ondiricana* (12th ed.)

Word of Sinta's single-handed apprehension of an astonishing seven armed robbers helped boost her credibility among the townspeople of Tenefir, enabling her to book a few new security commissions in the weeks to come. When Rilde brought snarling little Faika to her, however, to have the dog's charm refreshed, Sinta was shocked to learn that slanderous rumors were competing for currency with the truth. Evidently, Sinta was a woman of extremely loose morals, who, being fundamentally dishonest, as well, had borne false witness against innocent men and then used sorcery, as well as her feminine charms, to assure their prompt conviction and execution. No decent person could possibly consider hiring her.

Another three weeks went by before Othir returned to escort Sinta back to Sirigot for the second phase of enchanting Lord Pirendor's armor. Their journey was uneventful, providing Othir an opportunity to tell some highly entertaining (if perhaps somewhat embroidered) stories about his three maiden aunts, who appeared to have collectively exercised a despotic reign over his early childhood. "If they hadn't had my sisters and me to tyrannize," he concluded, "I have no doubt they would eventually have overthrown the duke himself and ruled jointly over the duchy in a sort of sororal condominium, purely as an outlet for their thwarted maidenly energies."

Sinta laughed. "A cautionary tale! I shall have to beware the uses to which I put my own."

Othir demurred. "I have no such concerns about you. Besides, should the occasion arise, you can always tyrannize Angvar."

The baron and baroness in Sirigot, while professing themselves pleased to see Sinta, seemed somewhat uncomfortable about something. Eventually they confessed to having heard the defamatory rumors about her. Perplexed, she did her best to ease their minds, supported by Othir, who felt he knew her well enough by now to vouch for her good character.

Fortunately, Sinta's work at Virt's went well. The armorer and his workers had duly crafted thousands of iron rings, but—following her instructions—they had yet to begin the extraordinarily time-consuming task of assembling them. On the afternoon of her arrival, Sinta kept her promise to Virt's wife and cast some useful household enchantments, but on the days that followed she devoted herself fully to the task at hand, casting a series of complex spells, not only to harden the rings, but also to rust-proof them, lubricate them, and reduce their apparent weight, so that the armor fashioned from them would encumber the wearer as little as possible. Making these spells permanent required a great deal of magical power, all but draining Sinta's *korethi* each day for six days running.

Each night she was visited anew by the two remaining wolves. Although she now found her voice at last, her stammering assertions that she was not afraid of bloodthirsty, savage lupines were singularly unconvincing, and neither creature showed any sign of believing a word of it. She found these dreams unnerving and woke each morning feeling apprehensive about their possible significance.

On the seventh day, escorted by Othir, Sinta returned to Tenefir, exhausted, but another 120 pendragons richer. They encountered few travelers of note, apart from an elaborate religious procession about an hour outside Sirigot. Some forty people, led by a group of priests in drab vestments Sinta did not recognize, paraded past, singing an aggressive-sounding hymn in an archaic form of Esdiric. She turned to Othir for enlightenment.

"The cult of Chigros," he explained, "an Esdiric holy man from before the Time of Troubles. He was reportedly extremely handsome, with a strong profile, dark hair and eyes, and a fine muscular physique."

Sinta smiled, both that her companion should consider these details worth mentioning and that they so closely matched his own appearance.

"Chigros was proselytizing in Hriss," Othir continued, "when he was murdered by Ondiric bandits. (We passed a stone marker earlier—I should have pointed it out to you.) In any case, according to legend, after the bandits chopped off his head, Chigros picked it up, put it back on his shoulders, and continued to preach for a good quarter of an hour before noticing that he was in fact dead. The bandits were appropriately astonished, and at least a few of them embraced this new faith and carried word of the alleged miracle back to his followers in Esdiron."

"And what were this holy man's theological views and moral teachings?" Sinta asked.

"Nothing out of the ordinary, and given his enforced absence they were soon largely forgotten anyway in favor of venerating his miraculous end."

Sinta rolled her eyes. She herself favored a hesitant deism, bordering on agnosticism, and the eccentricity of some of the world's more marginal religions never ceased to amaze her. "I see we have come to a stream," she remarked. "Let us water the horses."

Upon arriving in Tenefir, Sinta and Othir said their farewells at the livery stable, for Sinta wished to avoid overexciting Madam Imurga's romantic imagination. Her landlady, however, proved to have something weightier on her mind, having received word that Sinta's father, Talman the apothecary, had died of a stroke (or, as the message baldly described it, a "brain seizure") at his shop in Talindor, capital of the Principality of Sildoor. He was only forty-six.

The news came as a shock, and Sinta retreated to her room, where she wept quietly as the loss sank in. Although she had seen little of her father since beginning her magical apprenticeship at the age of thirteen, they had always been close. As his only child, she would have become his apprentice had the apothecaries' guild deigned to permit female membership. As it was, he had trained her as an apprentice in all but name up until the day Valdira offered to teach her sorcery instead.

Grieving aside, Sinta soon had to reckon with the practical consequences of her father's death. As his sole heir, she stood to inherit his shop, whatever the guild might think about the matter. Presumably her father's journeyman, Rolfar, could operate the business on her behalf, thus providing a modest stream of income, as she continued to make her way as a sorceress. She would, however, have to move back to Talindor and establish her practice there anew.

The next days were busy ones for the young sorceress, as she marshaled her belongings and decided what and how to pack. Her quarterstaff, of course, she would carry with her for self-protection. The same was true of the fine magic dagger she had acquired during her first year as an apprentice. Her enchanted money purse, with all her savings, would also remain on her person, as would the amulet she had taken from Grulfar and a bronze hairpin that Valdira had enchanted for her eighteenth birthday. The hairpin had the effect of magnifying the wearer's spell power by increasing the efficiency of her castings—much as a wand would have done, but more unobtrusively. Without it, enchanting the iron rings in Sirigot would have taken Sinta at least half again as long.

Of course, Angvar's magically self-cleaning travel basket was not to be forgotten. The indolent green lizard—like the knife, the former property of an odious necromancer—had grown considerably since coming into Sinta's life six years earlier, and she had been obliged to cast a spell of her own on the basket, so he would still fit inside. Sinta also obtained a small sack, in which she would carry a few personal treasures: a beautifully wrought golden diadem (albeit one whose previous owner was perhaps the most vicious tyrant in the history of the known world); an ancient gold coin (well over a thousand years old, with the head of a certain Queen Tissania on one side, and a dove of peace on the other); a tiny, beautifully faceted emerald (from the days before the art of gem-cutting had been lost); and a crudely carved wooden hedgehog (a toy from her childhood).

Even more precious were her parchment notes from seven years of magic study, consisting mostly of spells and the recipes for potions, coupled with a fair amount of theoretical material and learned commentary for consultation when she was devising new spells of her own. Obviously the notes were much too bulky to carry and therefore had to be packed. She had bound most of them herself into four hefty volumes with calfskin covers, though she had the foresight to have put the extensive notes relating to enchanting armor into a separate, smaller volume for ease of travel. Yet another volume contained the index she had painstakingly compiled, for the notes were chronological rather than thematic, and finding anything in them without a guide was a nightmare.

Sinta was also the proud owner of a rare copy of *Shengrod's Grimoire*—a parting gift from Valdira. Beautifully bound in fine red leather, with ornate brass clasps, it contained a wide range of wizarding spells, some of them very powerful. Further, a stack of loose materials represented seven years of arduous language study in the mystical tongues of both sorcery and wizardry, as well as the archaic Gantelic speech, and of course Tseren and Esdiric. Finally, she still had all her older, unbound apothecarial recipes, written in the archaic script the guild hoped would protect its secrets from nosy outsiders, such as herself.

All of these things required a great deal of space, so Sinta obtained a wooden crate from a nearby carpenter and enchanted it to be precisely as large on the inside as she needed it to be. As with her coin purse, she cast an additional spell to eliminate the extra weight.

The physical components for certain spells and the ingredients for potions she packed in a crate of their own, together with her medicaments and loose apothecarial ingredients, as well as their associated equipment, such as cauldrons of assorted sizes and a small mortar and pestle. Together, all these items took up considerably less room, however, than her nascent library, so with a little careful packing she was able to forgo enchanting the crate to increase its capacity. Both crates, however, she protected with a security spell, so that anyone attempting to break into them would receive a punch to the face from an invisible fist, after which a creepy, disembodied voice would quietly advise, "If I were you, I would run, while you still can!" Having in this way issued fair warning, the voice would then raise the alarm by screaming, "THIEF, THIEF, THIEF!" repeatedly.

Sinta did not bother with such precautions on the trunk she had brought with her to Tenefir, into which she now dumped her unimpressive collection of clothes, housewares, and toiletries. As previously noted, the young woman had her priorities.

7

Although many romantic tales are told of the pirates who preyed upon Ondiric merchant vessels prior to the rise of the Imperial Navy, in reality the predations of these sea-going criminals significantly hindered economic growth for centuries. Econometric analyses suggest that as much as 21.4 percent of Ondiric maritime trade was lost to piracy in the late medieval period, rising to 27.6 percent in the early modern era.

—*From Feudal Stagnation to Industrial Powerhouse: An Economic History of Ondiran*

The quickest and cheapest route from Tenefir to Talindor was via sailing ship to the port of Mindor and thence by riverboat up the Vassata. Admittedly, Sinta was even less comfortable with ocean travel than she was with riding on horseback, but she accepted that it was sometimes necessary. At the same time, her encounter with Grulfar and his band of robbers had reinforced her disinclination to journey by herself. A woman traveling alone, whatever her proficiency at self-defense, made too tempting a target. Fortunately, Sinta was not the only one with security concerns. Travelers of all sorts sought safety in numbers, traditionally looking to innkeepers to help them (for a modest fee) find others going in the same direction as themselves.

In this way, Sinta met an Esdiric couple with a new baby, who were headed up the coast. The husband, a journeyman stonemason, was hoping to find a job in Mindor, where an enormous Zoorist temple was under construction. Sinta found the couple, whose names were Dhirgos and Takhin, to be pleasant enough, and she was grateful for an opportunity to practice her Esdiric, which she knew needed work. The baby, like all babies in her experience, she found small, noisy, and thoroughly uninteresting.

Together, they booked passage on a stout oaken cog named the *Sunfish.* A fifty-foot, flat-bottomed, single-masted vessel of clinker construction, it was captained by an old Tseren seadog with a graying beard and a booming voice. He was not inclined to grant them a discount just because one of them purported to be a sorceress (even if she was unexpectedly fluent in Tseren), but when Sinta demonstrated her abilities by inducing his entire crew to temporarily abandon its duties, in favor of dancing a jig and singing a lugubrious sea shanty, he had to admit that such a spell would significantly reduce the threat posed by a crew of marauding pirates.

The ship was charted to hug the Ondiric coast, rounding the Risdaric peninsula to enter the channel separating the Continent from the island of Tserenets. After a stop to drop cargo at the Risdaric capital of Trovan, it would cross over to the Tseren port of Karandoz for the same purpose. The ship's course, as plotted, then called for it to cross back and follow the coast north the rest of the way to Mindor. Altogether, the expedition was expected to last six days, compared to a land journey of perhaps twelve. Admittedly, whether expectations would match reality was an open question.

⚜

When the day came for embarkation, Sinta went to the livery stable to rent a wagon and driver, as well as to retrieve the rouncey. She had chosen to name the horse Tamirandalia, which sounded poetic but was actually the Gantelic word for "thief-stomper." In the course of a campaign to win the mare's unensorcelled affection via kindness and a steady supply of delicious carrots, Sinta had herself grown fond of the animal. Having to transport a horse by ship was a nuisance, but she had no wish to leave this one behind.

Returning to Madam Imurga's, Sinta had the driver help her load her crates and trunk onto the wagon, then said goodbye to her landlady and the five rabbits. Madam Imurga shed a few tears but cheered up when she remembered that Tirresofis counseled joy upon parting, admittedly for reasons that remained obscure, due to a lacuna in the ancient text.

Sinta met Dhirgos and Takhin at the docks, where they loaded their baggage aboard the cog and arranged it in the crowded space allotted to them below decks. Tamirandalia was even more mistrustful of the cog than Sinta herself and took some coaxing to get aboard. As a precaution against rough seas, Sinta had the horse lie down, before then casting a sleep spell on her. She wished she could do the same for herself, but under the circumstances it seemed imprudent.

The first three days saw smooth sailing, though it took Sinta awhile to find her sea legs, making her feel ridiculous in the interim, while the unfortunate Dhirgos suffered from seasickness regardless of the easy passage. During the third night, however, the cog hit a summer squall that tossed it about like a toy boat in the bath of a rambunctious child, and abject terror reigned for several hours below decks. Sinta and Takhin joined Dhirgos in his nausea and vomiting, and Sinta expressed the hope that whoever had invented seafaring had ultimately drowned and was now adrift in an ocean of raging hellfire. She wished she knew something of witchcraft (one of the known world's other magic systems), for witches were widely believed to be able to control the weather. Since they were secretive as well as rare, however, Sinta could not be sure that these rumors about them were even true.

As dawn broke, it became apparent that the squall had driven the cog off course, and the captain had to admit (at least to himself) that he did not know where they were. All he could do was take his best guess and point the ship, winds permitting, in what he hoped to be the direction of the nearest land. He was still trying to get his bearings, however, when the sailor in the crow's nest reported a rapidly approaching vessel, very possibly piratical.

"Raise the sail—and get that damned sorceress up here!" shouted the captain, who quite reasonably felt that the fates were not, at present, treating him altogether fairly.

Sinta, who had only just succeeded in falling asleep, came on deck looking disheveled and feeling groggy. By this time the unknown ship had closed most of the distance between them, and the captain could see that it flew a black flag.

"Pirates!" he shouted at her. "Do something!"

Sinta felt a jolt of fear but did not let it stop her from turning to face in the direction the captain was pointing, while the crew around her struggled to get the cog underway. "I have to wait until they're closer," she told him, watching apprehensively as the ship approached. Even from this distance she could see pirates on deck, brandishing their weapons.

"They're almost on us," the captain shouted, when the ship had closed to within a hundred yards. "Do something quick, or they'll be feeding us to the sharks!"

A sleepless night, enlivened by fear, nausea, and vomiting, had done nothing to restore Sinta's *korethi.* On the contrary, it had resulted in a further depletion. The sorceress therefore had to choose her spell carefully. In the end, she conjured a fireball, about an inch in diameter, and sent it skimming across the water. As it approached the pirate ship, it climbed sharply and exploded some fifteen feet above the deck in a tightly controlled blast. There were screams, and several of the pirates threw themselves quite unnecessarily against the deck, but no one was hurt. To be sure, Sinta had not intended to kill pirates, but rather to set fire to the square-rigged sail of their ship, and she was gratified to see that by focusing all of the spell's energy so tightly, she had succeeded in getting the canvas to ignite. As fire gradually engulfed the entire sail, the ship slowed until it was dead in the water, even as the cog began to pull away. The rising flames forced one pirate, who was trapped on the yardarm, to leap clumsily into the sea, while the boy in the crow's nest executed a more dignified swan dive.

"Threat dealt with," Sinta told the captain a trifle smugly. "Now, if you have nothing further, I'm going back to my nest of old rope and worn-out blankets."

Fortunately, the captain's instincts pointed him in the right direction, and the cog arrived at Trovan having lost a mere twelve hours. Sinta woke Tamirandalia for some much-needed exercise, and together they went ashore with Dhirgos and Takhin, while the crew unloaded cargo. The changing tide, the captain warned, required a quick turnaround.

Having never ventured into the County of Risdar before, Sinta was eager to learn more about the place. She knew that the population of the peninsula spoke a language closely related to Tseren and mostly followed an old religion called Roonthan. She had also heard rumors that witchcraft was practiced in many of the isolated villages of the hilly interior. Trovan (or Zerifendets, as it was known in Risdaric) itself turned out to be little more than an over-grown fishing village dominated by the forbidding granite castle of the ruling count. The stench of fish being dried, smoked, and salted wherever one looked was pervasive and overwhelming.

Their legs not yet readjusted to dry land, the visitors stumbled through the muddy streets in search of an apothecary's shop, where they might seek a remedy for Dhirgos's seasickness. Asking for directions, Sinta found that she could usually make herself understood in Tseren, though she could not always follow the Risdaric answers she received in return. At length, however, she did succeed in leading her companions to a small and poorly supplied shop, where she requested some chamomile flowers, which she assured them would mitigate Dhirgos's nausea. The apothecary, a surly fellow who had not shaved recently, regarded with suspicion the mixture of Esdiric and Hrissic currency Takhin offered him, but he finally accepted it, after a certain amount of unmistakable, if incomprehensible, grumbling.

On their way back to the cog, Sinta treated the others to a snack of smoked eel from a street vendor. Or at least she intended for it to be a treat, since smoked eel was considered a delicacy in much of Ondiran. To her disappointment, the two Esdir eyed the desiccated, leathery, saltwater creatures with a suspicion fully equal to that the apothecary had shown their foreign coins. In the end, however, having little choice but to try the eels, they admitted the flavor was quite agreeable and even bought a few more to eat later.

❦

Returning to the wharf, the travelers were alarmed to discover that a fierce brawl had broken out between the crew of the cog and that of a larger vessel flying the flag of the northern Duchy of Trusilor. They never did learn what the quarrel was about, but anyone could see that the crew of the cog, outnumbered ten to six, would soon be so badly pummeled it would not be able to sail the ship. Indeed, as they approached, the boatswain was taking a savage kicking from two of the northerners, while the much bloodied ship's cook was about to be thrown into the bay. The two captains were exchanging abuse at the tops of their lungs in Tseren and Ondiric, and a large northern sailor was chasing down the cog's youngest crewman, a lad of perhaps fourteen, with a boathook, leaving him no escape except to dive into the murky water.

"Do something, Sinta," pleaded Takhin. "You're a sorceress. Use your powers!"

Realizing that the situation was too chaotic to be contained by directing her magicks at the scattered northern crewmen, Sinta concluded that she needed to seize their chain of command instead and give it a firm yank. She began with the spell that had so impressed the western sailors back in Tenefir and threw a handful of multicolored sparks between the two angry captains, just to get their attention. "Enough!" she shouted, in a voice she scarcely recognized as her own. "End this melee, or by all the demons that haunt your dreams, I shall end it for you!"

The northern captain, a stocky, weather-beaten man with one ear missing and a brass hoop earring in the other, laughed scornfully. "That's big talk from such a little girl," he scoffed. "My men will end this all right—by beating those bastards bloody. D'you really want a piece of that?"

Sinta pursed her lips nervously, aware that if all the northern crewmen should rush her at once, she would be hard pressed to fend them off. But she was committed now. She answered the captain with a gesture that levitated him some six feet in the air and flipped him upside down. "End it," she told him, "or I'll drop you on your head." She took a deep breath. "Vex me further, and I'll burn your ship down to the waterline, as well."

It was the Tseren captain's turn to laugh. "She can do it, too," he advised. "There's a crew of pirates off the southern coast who can tell you that!"

The northern captain squirmed and flailed in mid-air, trying without success to right himself. "Put me down, damn you!"

Sinta shook her head and gestured him another four feet higher. "I don't think so." She scuffed the wooden planks of the wharf with the toe of her shoe. "Feels like hardwood to me. Oak perhaps? A nasty fall to take, anyway." With a single rotation of one upraised finger, she threw him into a dizzying spin. "Tell your men to stand down and return to your ship."

By now the fighting had largely ceased, as the sailors on both sides stopped to gawk at the spectacle of an upended sea captain spinning like a top ten feet in the air.

At this point the unhappy man had no alternative but to admit defeat. "You heard her," he bellowed. "Do it!"

Sinta ceased his spinning but waited until both crews were safely aboard their respective vessels before dropping him headfirst into the water. She turned to the grizzled Tseren seafarer. "Ready to cast off, Captain?"

He grinned. "Aye, aye, miss!"

⸙

Back onboard, Sinta opened the crate containing her apothecary supplies to supplement the ship's meager medical provisions, as the *Sunfish* resumed its course. Since the ship's cook doubled rather haphazardly as the ship's surgeon, she began by treating his injuries. Together they then tended to the other battered members of the crew, with a little help from Takhin, while Dhirgos looked after the baby.

⸙

It took them another day to reach Karandoz. Having visited the city before, Sinta knew it to be a thriving commercial center. She therefore led her companions and Tamirandalia through the dock district, with its taverns and brothels, into the city center, where the daily market was underway. Dhirgos and Takhin had little cash to spare, but they were interested in seeing all the goods for sale, while Sinta was pleased to find some useful ingredients to purchase, particularly a rare magical herb that sorcerers called *fithgit,* wizards called *fotgoss,* and apothecaries knew by its Gantelic name, *fetgutius.* In addition to its magical properties, it was helpful in the treatment of male-pattern baldness, and Sinta felt confident that her newly inherited shop would profit from obtaining an ample supply. A tedious negotiation ensued to determine how many Hrissic silver griffins Sinta should pay in place of the demanded quantity of Tseren silver *izgöttek,* but she eventually wore the seller down and received a favorable price and a handful of small change, as well.

"Gimme coin, rich lady!" whined a small beggar child who had caught wind of the transaction. With its tangled hair and muddy face, Sinta would have been hard pressed to say whether it was a boy or a girl. Whatever compassion she might have felt for the filthy creature, however, she knew perfectly well that if she complied with its demand, a small army of beggar children would besiege her for the next half hour at least, grabbing at her skirts and screeching for alms.

She shook her head. "Go away!"

Tamirandalia appeared to share her sentiments and nickered disapprovingly at the tiny brat.

"Gimme coin, rich lady!" importuned the beggar child with the air of one who can go on until doomsday.

Not all the skills Sinta had learned from Valdira fell within the ambit of sorcery, and the art of legerdemain was one of her favorites. Even as she cast a charm spell and touched a finger to the side of her nose, she used her other hand to conceal upon the young urchin's person a rusty Tseren iron piece, worth, she reckoned, perhaps half a Fendoric farthing. "Now, go!" she ordered and watched with relief as the beggar child wandered off, looking dazed, but none the wiser.

❦

Enjoying favorable winds, the rest of the voyage to Mindor was uneventful, apart from the sighting of a pod of whales. Sinta had never seen these spectacular creatures before, so naturally she had a great many questions about them, some of which the captain could actually answer, having taken part in Tseren whale hunts as a young man. Sinta was particularly interested to learn that these behemoths were not fish, but mammals. It was the sort of seemingly inconsequential fact she liked to file away in the back of her brain, awaiting the day when it might somehow prove useful.

Upon arrival in Mindor, Sinta took leave of her fellow travelers, wishing Dhirgos well with his stonemasonry and Takhin with her childrearing. She then had the prompt good fortune to find a river barge with a small party of passengers to which she could attach herself. Tamirandalia got to walk on the towpath with the mules as they pulled the barge upstream, an arrangement she vastly preferred to coming aboard. All in all, Sinta herself was quite content, and within another three days she was back in Talindor, the place of her birth.

8

The picturesque city of Talindor, capital of the former Principality of Sildoor in the post-Unification province of Sindegorn, is overlooked by a fine castle built in the early Rendiric style, albeit with spurious later additions. Although the steep hill must be ascended on foot, as no motor-parking has yet been arranged above, the castle is well worth a visit, if only for the panoramic view (purchase tickets at the lower gatehouse *before* ascending). The artificial fruit and flower museum will perhaps be of interest to some.

—*The Motor-Tourist's Guide to Ondiran* (3rd ed.)

Over a year had passed since Sinta had last been in Talindor, visiting her father on her way to investigate a potential job in Hriss after she finished her apprenticeship. Little seemed to have changed, however, since her childhood, when she actually lived there. Although Talindor enjoyed the imperial privilege of calling itself a city, it was in reality scarcely more than a large town. Clinging to the steep left bank of the Vassata, it lay opposite the prince's castle, which stood on a hill rising abruptly from the right bank. Economically stagnant, the town showed no signs of expanding beyond the walls that had been slowly rebuilt after the devastation of the Time of Troubles five centuries earlier.

Stopping at a livery stable convenient to the riverside docks, Sinta boarded Tamirandalia, hired two porters to carry her crates, and cast a spell to levitate her trunk. The apothecary's shop, located on the main square, was not far (for nothing in Talindor was very far, though the climb to get there might be arduous). Upon reaching it, the porters set down the two crates and watched as Sinta brought her trunk gently to ground.

No one answered the sorceress's knock. It was early evening, after closing time, and she surmised that Rolfar the journeyman, Ghir the apprentice, and Ferga the housekeeper and cook, must all be off entertaining themselves. Having no key, Sinta bypassed the security spells she had installed on a previous visit, after which she was able to unlock the door safely by magic. The porters took her crates inside, received their pay, and left. She then levitated her trunk inside, as well, and stepped into the dark windowless shop herself.

After casting a spell to illuminate the ceiling, Sinta took a look around. The walls to the left and right were lined with built-in, floor-to-ceiling pigeonholes, each containing a different rare ingredient, all labeled in her father's calligraphic rendition of apothecarial script. The narrow back wall was covered with broad shelves bearing row after row of ceramic jars containing the more common dry ingredients and some glass bottles with the liquid ones. On the sales counter stood a well-used mortar and pestle, as well as a small brass balance, with its accompanying set of tiny brass weights. The counter's drawers, Sinta knew, held the most frequently requested medications, already prepared and packaged for sale. A small stove stood in one corner of the room, along with several glass beakers, three nested copper cauldrons, and a small alembic. The blue-and-white tiled floor now had more cracks than she remembered, and the low, wooden ceiling was even blacker with soot from the shop's oil lamps, though this fact was obscured by her light spell. Turning, Sinta saw that the exterior wall was still decorated with the same faded, life-sized diagrams of human anatomy she had studied as a child, with their detailed annotations regarding the afflictions to which different body parts were prone and the correct treatments to be applied to each.

Inhaling the familiar scent of dried herbs, stale lamp smoke, and medicinal alcohol, Sinta was carried back to the fateful day when Valdira strode into the shop, looking regal in a high-waisted azure dress embroidered with silver thread. Behind the counter, in defiance of guild rules, thirteen-year-old Sinta had hastened to ready the unusual and aromatic unguent demanded by this aristocratic creature, whose piercing gray-blue eyes fixed upon her with ever-increasing intensity as the work progressed. Sinta had no way of knowing it at the time, but an experienced magician can sense magical power in others, and Valdira had picked up on the girl's potential.

The stranger paid for her purchase with some Fendoric silver. "Hold out your hand!" she commanded afterward. Sinta was too frightened not to obey, besides which—unlikely though it seemed—a tip could perhaps be in the offing. Instead the woman produced a wand from her pocket and tapped Sinta's hand with it, causing the girl's entire body briefly to luminesce, in what Sinta now knew had been a confirmation of her magical power. For a terrifying split second, she could actually see through the flesh of her own hand, to the complicated configuration of delicate bones within.

"I need to speak with your father," said the woman in a voice that brooked no argument.

Sinta hastened to fetch him, and a long conference ensued in the back room, a conference from which she was excluded, notwithstanding her intense curiosity about it.

"This is the Lady Valdira," her father told her when the two reemerged. "She is a sorceress of renown and has expressed a willingness to take you on as an apprentice at her home in Fendor. I have to say, my girl, that as much as I would hate to lose you, this is an extraordinary opportunity. I don't think you should pass it up."

"Your father assures me that you are both diligent and clever," Valdira told her, "which is fortunate, because if you accept my offer, you will have to study extremely hard. Sorcery is no avocation for lazybones or dummies, and I am *not* a patient mistress." She paused. "In addition to room and board, you will receive one Fendoric penny a week in pocket money, subject to forfeiture if you break anything or otherwise annoy me." Her gaze grew even more penetrating. "What say you, girl? Do you have the ambition and drive to become a sorceress?"

Sinta's thirst for knowledge contended with her characteristic timidity in a fierce struggle for supremacy.

Somewhat panic-stricken, she looked from Valdira to her father, and back again …

⚜

The sound of a key turning in the lock interrupted Sinta's reverie.

"Oh, so *you're* here, are you?" Rolfar did not sound pleased, but then he had never had much time for his employer's precocious offspring. Eighteen years her senior, he really should have been a master himself by now. Whether he had failed the guild's strict examinations, or there was simply a dearth of openings available to those journeymen who had passed them, Sinta did not know. She supposed the vacancy created by her father's death might soon reveal the answer.

"Hello, Rolfar," she said, trying to be pleasant. "Where are Ghir and Ferga?"

Rolfar scowled. "The guild reassigned Ghir to a shop in Brix, where he could continue his apprenticeship under the guidance of a master." (Sinta noted that this seemed to answer her question about Rolfar's status.) "Ferga is away visiting her sister. She seemed to need some time off."

"Very sensible," Sinta said. She knew Ferga would have found the apothecary's sudden death upsetting. She was not sure Rolfar had. "How's business?" she asked after an awkward pause.

Rolfar grunted irritably. "How is it ever? We sell enough to get by."

Beginning to find this conversation trying, Sinta cast about for a topic that might mollify the surly journeyman.

"Well, I'll need you to run the shop for me now. That will mean an increase in responsibility, so I'll try to manage a corresponding increase in pay—though until I've had a chance to look at the books, I can't be sure how much it will be."

Rolfar shrugged. "The guild may have something to say about that."

Sinta sighed. "So they might. There's very little the guild does not have something to say about, especially if one is fool enough to ask them."

Seeing little point in continuing to chat with Rolfar in his present mood, Sinta made her way through the back room to the kitchen to see if, in Ferga's absence, she could locate something to eat. Evidently Rolfar was procuring his meals elsewhere, for there was little to be found beyond some stale rye bread, upon which Sinta gnawed distractedly, as she went upstairs. She had no wish to reoccupy her old attic room—until recently Ghir's—for it was small and cramped, as well as hot during the summer, but at the same time she found the prospect of moving into her father's bedchamber a little unsettling. She went in anyway, hoping to get accustomed to the idea, only to find herself confronted with the bed in which, presumably, she had been conceived, and in which, quite certainly, her mother had died giving birth to her. The other furnishings were rather sparse: an old wardrobe with her father's few spare clothes; a small table with a wash basin, water jug, and chamber pot; a garland of dried flowers hanging from a nail on the wall near the window. Her mother, her father had once confided, wore those flowers on their wedding day, and they were all he had, apart from Sinta herself, to remember her by.

She made her decision. Tonight she would sleep in the stuffy attic. Tomorrow she would go out and buy a new bed.

9

Certain smaller guilds were organized regionally, rather than municipally. The Apothecaries' Guild of Sindegorn, for example, comprised twenty shops in sixteen cities and towns across nine nominally sovereign political entities. Headquartered in Ool, it sometimes struggled to police its geographically dispersed membership.

—*The Encyclopædia Ondiricana* (12th ed.)

Settling into the shop in Talindor and defending her inheritance consumed most of Sinta's time and energy for the coming weeks, leaving distressingly little opportunity for sorcery. Unpacking her belongings should have been easy, but she had trouble deciding how best to integrate them into the existing clutter of her father's study, much of which was essential to the continued operation of the shop downstairs. The extradimensional crate proved useful for storage, while the second crate—with a few modifications—made a good nesting box for Angvar, replacing a smaller one she had left behind in Tenefir. Reviewing the shop's books to get a sense of its true financial condition was both time-consuming and dull, while supervising Rolfar, who remained sullen and resentful, was both time-consuming and stressful. Ferga's absence was also a source of tension, but once she returned from her sister's, she was a great help in managing the household.

Talman had made an iron-clad will, leaving everything to his daughter (apart from minor bequests to Ferga, Rolfar, and a mysterious woman named Lia), but vindicating Sinta's legal rights still proved to be an ordeal. She was fortunate that the Principality of Sildoor was one of the few Ondiric jurisdictions that permitted women to inherit property at all, but the municipal officials in Talindor seemed to regard the erection of bureaucratic obstacles as their sacred duty. In the end, she felt compelled to cast charm spells on a number of them to ease the way, particularly when dealing with ones who hinted that they were expecting bribes.

Sinta's main source of anxiety, however, was the apothecaries' guild. While it could not prevent her from inheriting the shop, it did have the power to stymie her operation of it. From the guild's point of view, the shop existed to provide a living for a master apothecary, not some know-it-all sorceress. The guild could, if it chose, extract Rolfar, as it had Ghir, leaving her with no qualified personnel. It could sponsor a rival shop in town and drive her out of business. Even if it did neither of these things, it could make her life miserable in any number of minor ways through constant interference in the shop's affairs. The question, really, was how would the guild choose to make up its collective mind?

Auditors came to Talindor to inspect the shop, interview Rolfar, and interrogate Sinta. They were followed weeks later by various other guildsmen, who did much the same without any explanation. Finally, Sinta received a summons to report to the guild hall in Ool to meet with the guild master, though to what end, she could only speculate.

❧

Ool was but a four-hour ride away. Why the guild hall should be located there, rather than in one of the more important cities in the region, had never been clear to Sinta, but corruption seemed the most likely explanation. In any event, she rented a horse for Rolfar, so that he could accompany her and Tamirandalia. After all, if a decision were finally to be reached, it would affect him, too. The summer weather was sultry, and the riders were soon pestered by biting insects. Fortunately, Sinta remembered a spell to discourage them, a feat that helped improve Rolfar's humor considerably. Even so, conversation remained limited, for Sinta was preoccupied with the meeting to come.

The princely city of Ool was an even quieter town than Talindor, which at least had river traffic to encourage trade, but the guild hall on the main square was an imposing structure, quite new and built according to the latest architectural fashion. "Nice to know where our guild dues have been going," observed Rolfar, as they dismounted and he took charge of the horses. He hesitated. "Good luck," he said, finally, as Sinta climbed the steps to the ornate bronze entrance doors.

She turned and smiled at him. "Thank you, Rolfar. Good luck to us both!"

❧

Tilven, the guild master, was a diminutive man in his mid-sixties, with thin white hair and bulging eyes of the palest possible blue. He began the interview by expressing his condolences to Sinta on the loss of her father. "He was an excellent apothecary, and a good man. I know he was proud of you."

Sinta bowed her head. "I am proud to have been his daughter."

Tilven expressed regret (and possibly a hint of criticism) that Sinta had been unable to attend the funeral (for which the guild had paid, including for the sermon by a Cantiferian minister, though the deceased had been a lapsed Asardian). He then moved on to the matter at hand. The other master apothecaries, he told her, were evenly divided, nine to nine, leaving the deciding vote in his hands. "It is a testament to the high regard in which your father's fellows held him that so many desire to respect his wishes, even though from the point of view of guild law and precedent, it would be highly irregular to place the business in the hands of an outsider."

Sinta sensed a certain annoyance behind Tilven's polite phrases. He was not on her side.

"So, as I said," Tilven continued, "the deciding vote is *mine alone.*" He gave her a significant look. "You *are* a pretty little thing, aren't you!"

Sinta gritted her teeth. She had not intended to bring magic into this negotiation, but if Tilven wanted to play dirty, so be it. She silently cast a spell and touched the side of her nose. "Whether I am or not, you *will* vote in my favor, Guild Master!"

Tilven's face contorted as he fought to resist the charm. "Faugh!" he exclaimed at last. "No, I don't think so, you spell-casting hussy." His face twisted into a sneer. "That's right—I've heard all about *you!*"

Seething, Sinta uttered a short incantation and watched Tilven's pasty white face turn crimson and sweat begin pouring down his brow, as though he were in a dangerously overheated sauna. "I would urge you to reconsider, Guild Master. I don't want you and your guild arrayed against me, but that is a road that runs in both directions. Trust me, Guild Master: you don't want to run afoul of a sorceress. Don't delude yourself on that point, just because you can resist a simple charm spell."

Panting, Tilven struggled to remove the little ruff he was wearing around his neck.

"You seem warm, Guild Master." Sinta gestured sharply with one hand, canceling the spell. She then uttered a new incantation, however, and watched Tilven turn even paler than he had been to begin with, as he shivered violently with cold. "Better?" she asked sardonically. She sighed. "Perhaps not." Having made her point, she canceled the new spell with the same curt gesture, and folded her arms defiantly. "It seems to me, Guild Master, that it is in both our interests to reach some equitable compromise. Don't you agree?"

Chastened, Tilven conceded that she might be right, and negotiations began afresh on that basis.

Well over two hours later, Sinta emerged from the guild house. Rolfar was waiting across the square, resting with the two horses in the shade of a plane tree.

“I’m sorry,” she told him. “You will be working under a new master, after all: one Pentigor, up to now a journeyman in Mar-Beran. Do you know him?”

Rolfar did not seem surprised. “We’ve met. But what about you? Did the guild succeed in ridding itself of you?”

Sinta grimaced. “Not quite. I’m selling the business and its inventory to Pentigor, but I’m keeping the building, so he will be my tenant.”

They mounted the horses. Sinta rode quietly, reflecting on the deal she had just struck. She was inclined to think that things had ultimately worked out for the best. Not only had she insisted upon a good price, but Rolfar’s grumpiness and the guild’s interference would be Pentigor’s problems now, leaving her free to devote herself to sorcery. And she would have sufficient resources to do so without being dependent on spoiled clients looking for lost dogs.

10

Dating back to early medieval times, the harvest festival known as Vendritan is one of Talindor's most charming traditions. Peasants from the surrounding countryside, dressed in their quaint folk costumes, parade through the streets, cheered on by the townspeople. Come evening, a huge public feast is held, followed by fireworks. Formerly sponsored by the prince, the festival is now funded from the municipal coffers. Everyone is in a merry mood, and no one goes home hungry!

—*Beautiful Talindor: An Illustrated Guide for Visitors*

While the household awaited Pentigor's arrival, Sinta had to decide whether to move out or to rearrange accommodations within the house. After giving the matter due consideration, she chose to relinquish her father's bedchamber and study to Pentigor, and move her things to the floor above, where there was an empty room, with a window onto the square, that might serve as a study, as well as two smaller rooms stuffed floor-to-ceiling with miscellaneous rubbish. Her father's predecessor had been a packrat, and when he died, everything had been pushed into those upstairs rooms, along with anything further, over time, that seemed to belong there. Cleaning out at least one of them would give Sinta a place to sleep.

In the end, she emptied both rooms, doing most of the work herself, with the help of levitation spells for the heavier items. Moving her father's bed back to its original location made a start, followed by an extended process of sorting. She found an old desk in reasonably good condition that could go into her new study, along with a broken chair and a pretty vase with a hairline crack, both of which she repaired by magic. There was also a sort of iron dingbat, to which she took a perverse liking. She had no idea what purpose it might once have served, but it was ugly in a way that somehow appealed to her, so she moved it into her study, as well. Rolfar found one or two small items that he wanted, and Ferga took a tin washtub that looked usable, but the remaining three wagonloads Sinta sold to a local junk dealer for a small sum. She then moved her new bed into the larger of the two rooms, along with her mother's wedding garland and Angvar's new nesting box. A few other necessary items of furniture she bought second-hand.

❦

By the terms of her contract with the guild, all her father's apothecarial recipes belonged to Pentigor, so Sinta stayed up late each night before he arrived, copying out those she did not already have. In the process she discovered two letters she had sent her father at the very beginning of her apprenticeship. Written in apothecarial script for privacy, they conveyed equal parts apprehension and wonder, as she first entered the world of sorcery. She now quietly took possession of them and resumed her copying.

Pentigor, when he ultimately arrived, proved to be an unremarkable-looking man of thirty-two. Reticent at first, he became positively voluble when Sinta engaged him on the topic of certain medicinal herbs. He demonstrated the depth of knowledge one might expect from a master apothecary, coupled with a boyish enthusiasm more common (though far from universal) in an apprentice. Sinta decided that she liked him, while Rolfar and Ferga reserved judgment.

Six days later, Pentigor's new bride, a russet-haired young woman named Ghisende, came to join him. Notwithstanding the considerable mortgage debt to the guild and the monthly rent to Sinta, Pentigor's elevation to master had finally given him the security to wed, after an engagement that had lasted more than six years. Ghisende, however, regarded Sinta with instinctive mistrust and immediately clashed with Ferga, but she was a nice enough person at heart, who would adjust to the other members of the household over time, and they to her.

One week before the autumnal equinox, Sinta received a summons to the castle. Simultaneously intrigued and alarmed, she changed into her best dress and fetched Tamirandalia from the livery stable. "We're wanted at court," she explained, as she saddled the horse, "if you can imagine such a thing."

The castle's lower gatehouse stood at the far end of the long graceful stone bridge spanning the river. The guards examined Sinta's summons and let her pass. The steep road on the other side was dominated along its entire length by an adjacent covered gallery, built deep into the side of the hill, so that the castle's garrison could direct murderous defensive fire against anyone foolish enough to hazard this line of attack.

Guards at the upper gatehouse, near the top of the ascent, examined Sinta's summons anew. Instructing her to wait, they summoned a groom, who accompanied her across a large courtyard to the stables, where she parted company with Tamirandalia. A footman then escorted her through yet another gate into a smaller courtyard and finally into the primary structure of the castle itself. Several grand halls and corridors later, she was presented to a courtier, who bade her to wait in an antechamber, while he informed the prince's chancellor of her arrival. Within minutes she was then called into the latter's august presence.

The chancellor was an elderly man, physically frail but with alert, intelligent eyes. His clothes were uncommonly rich, and he wore a heavy chain of office around his shoulders. "You are a sorceress?" he demanded, wasting no time on formalities.

Sinta confirmed that she was.

"You are very young."

Sinta shrugged. "And yet, I am fully trained."

"By Valdira of Fendoran, I believe?"

Sinta nodded.

"That inspires more confidence," the chancellor admitted.

"As it should," Sinta replied. "She is a magician of great power and intellect."

"Indeed," said the chancellor, gesturing for her to be seated. "You are perhaps aware that the prince's own magician, the sorcerer Bentilan, recently lost his grip on reality and is now quite insane?"

Sinta had to admit that she had not known this.

"Yes, it is a very sad case, but at least he does not appear to be dangerous, for he believes himself to be a badger with no magical powers. We think it had something to do with some new spell he was working on, but we cannot really be sure."

Sinta expressed suitable regret and sympathy. It was sobering to be reminded that magic-use had its dangers, even for a practiced hand.

The chancellor sighed. "Naturally, we are searching for a replacement. A man with many years' experience, of course."

"Of course," Sinta echoed drily, before she could stop herself.

The chancellor chose to overlook her tone. "In the meantime, we are without a sorcerer to prepare the pyrotechnic display for Vendritan. You are familiar with the festival? But, of course, you are—you are a native daughter of Talindor." The chancellor looked at her searchingly. "But are pyrotechnic displays in your line? I would imagine they might be a somewhat narrow specialty."

Sinta had to admit that she had never put on such a display. "But I am of course familiar with the spells involved. With sufficient forethought and preparation, I'm sure I could put together a creditable performance."

The chancellor looked skeptical. "You have a week."

⁂

Having considerably exaggerated her pyrotechnic skills, Sinta returned home in something of a panic after securing the lucrative commission. She knew how to throw fireballs, of course, and she had a vague recollection that by adding certain physical spell components, the flames could be made to appear in different colors. She could also use her spark-throwing spell. With the exertion of enough *korethi,* no doubt it could be quite impressive. But the more elaborate displays that she remembered from the Vendritan celebrations of her childhood must have been based on spells she did not know.

A rummage through her notes confirmed that a pinch of rose madder would turn a fireball red, while indigo would turn it blue. These could be mixed together, or with yellow sulfur, to achieve other colors in various shades, or one could resort to oxidized copper for green, or the shells of certain mollusks for purple, or lapis lazuli for ultramarine. Of course, most of these ingredients were expensive and hard to come by at short notice. It occurred to her, however, that if the chancellor would grant her access to Bentilan's workshop, she might find stocks left over from previous years. Better still, by searching his library, she might learn how to cast some of the more spectacular spells. This thought reminded her to consult her copy of *Shengrod's Grimoire,* but all she found there was a spell to call down lightning during a storm, an effect that—while impressive—seemed of limited usefulness at a festival.

Fortunately, the chancellor saw the value of letting her into Bentilan's alarmingly cluttered rooms. Not only did she find healthy supplies of madder, indigo, and sulfur, but there were smaller quantities of powdered copper and purple mollusk, as well. It took hours of searching, but she also found and carefully copied out several pyrotechnic spells, plus one or two other enchantments that had nothing to do with the matter at hand, but which she could not resist.

The remaining days before the festival Sinta spent planning a display she hoped would not embarrass her. She made repeated visits to the countryside, where she could practice the new spells and experiment with different effects without drawing the sort of attention she would have garnered in town. Luckily, the pyrotechnic spells she had found among Bentilan's belongings included his own annotations, with recommendations for increased efficiency, so that casting them would expend the least possible *korethi.* If Sinta were to produce a display of any duration and complexity, these hints would be crucial. Indeed, further to this purpose, she had an idea to enhance her fireballs, though she needed some expert advice to establish its feasibility.

Sinta was lucky that Talindor had a resident alchemist, for it was not the most common of professions. The climb to his shop was a steep one, and she was winded by the time she got there. While catching her breath, she took a moment to admire the view of the town below and the castle on the opposing hill. It was a useful reminder of the scale on which she would have to work if she hoped to impress an audience accustomed to Bentilan's productions.

Though the alchemist had been a friend of her father's, Sinta had always thought him a bit peculiar (though perhaps no more peculiar, in retrospect, than any of the other alchemists she had encountered since). He was about her father's age, but a life spent working with dangerous chemicals had not been kind to him. His skin showed several unflattering discolorations, and he was missing two fingers from his left hand.

"Good morning, Master Dvortin," Sinta said, performing one of her better curtsies. The shop had an acrid, smoky odor, but she managed to avoid coughing.

"Good morning, miss," the alchemist replied a little woodenly. He had not seen her in at least seven years and did not appear to recognize her.

Sinta got straight to the point. "What can you tell me about black powder?"

He gave her an odd look. Evidently young women did not come to him with such questions often. "It goes bang. What more do you need to know?"

Sinta suppressed an eye roll. "What kind of bang? Just how explosive is it? I need a big flash."

Dvortin looked at her more closely. "Wait a minute. You're Talman's girl, aren't you? The one who went away to become a sorceress. I heard you were back in town." He cracked a painful smile. "What do you want a big flash for, anyway?"

Sinta explained her idea.

Dvortin shook his head. "No, black powder's not what you want. Burns too slow and makes too much smoke. No, clubmoss spores are what you need."

Sinta stared at him. "Clubmoss spores? We use them to treat urinary disorders!"

Dvortin gave a dry, barking laugh that in another context might have been a cough. "Maybe so, but set them alight and BANG, you've got yourself a big flash all right, with very little heat or smoke." He demonstrated with a pinch of powder from a jar behind the counter.

Sinta bought all the clubmoss spores he had, before going home and raiding her shop—or rather, Pentigor's shop—for its supply, as well. "I'm buying these," she told Pentigor, "and I need you to get me more, a lot more! Tell the guild I'm paying double the retail price for all the clubmoss spores they can lay their hands on, as long as they get them to me before the festival. After that, no deal."

Pentigor gave her a puzzled look. "Are you all right, Sinta?"

She laughed. "I'm fine. Don't worry—I don't actually have history's worst bladder infection!"

A week was not really enough time to put together a first-rate pyrotechnic display, but as the day of the equinox dawned and the sun rose due east for the first time in half a year, Sinta felt reasonably sure that she could put on a show that would at least be acceptable, so long as she kept her head and did not make any stupid mistakes in its execution.

She reported to the castle early, before the festival could crowd the streets with revelers and make movement difficult. The chancellor's clerk escorted her to the roof of the tallest tower, where she unpacked her supplies. In truth, she had not yet perfected her plans, and being on the spot would help her make last-minute choices about how to choreograph her performance.

By mid-morning hundreds of peasants were flooding into the city in their festive costumes. From Sinta's vantage point in the tower, they looked like so many brightly colored ants. She watched the ebb and flow of the crowd through the streets and reflected that the individual participants doubtless had no notion of the complex rhythms of motion in which they were collectively engaged, notwithstanding how apparent those were when seen from a distance.

Sinta had brought a small picnic lunch with her. While she ate, she watched the mayor of Talindor give a speech from a balcony on the town hall. He was too far away for her to hear what he said, but it appeared to go over well with the revelers assembled on the town square. At any rate, their cheers were loud enough to reach the castle tower. Later, as the hour approached for the great evening feast, the prince addressed a gathering of his subjects on the bridge from atop the lower gatehouse. Sinta could not hear what he said, either, but she knew from childhood that he was a poor speaker and that the main thrust of his remarks would be to remind everyone just whose generosity had paid for it all. Once he was finished, the feast began to be served up from ten large open-air kitchens, set up around the city. This system of decentralized distribution was an attempt to mitigate the very real danger of this moment. The year before Sinta was born, there had been a stampede on the town square, and six people were trampled to death. No one wanted a repetition of that!

Before long, the chancellor's clerk climbed back up the tower to invite Sinta to partake of the castle's feast, which she gladly did. Vendritan was an opportunity for the bakers' guild to shine, for the holiday traditionally featured a variety of fancy specialty breads to celebrate the harvest. Sinta had not had an opportunity to enjoy most of them since leaving for her apprenticeship. Of less interest to her, the town's two breweries competed fiercely each year to see which one would give away more free beer (courtesy of the prince), enabling it to acclaim its brew as the popular favorite.

Sinta trudged back up the tower's long spiraling stairs, having eaten—in addition to the various breads—perhaps too many servings of veal, boar, venison, and swan. The residents of the castle, it must be admitted, enjoyed a richer feast than did the rest of the populace. She was joined on the roof by both the chancellor (wheezing alarmingly from the exertion) and his clerk, along with two men they introduced to her as the prince's falconer and the keeper of the princely seal. Before long, two minor courtiers appeared, as well, accompanied by two ladies-in-waiting, with whom they were obviously carrying on an illicit flirtation. Sinta wished they would all go away, though she soon came to appreciate that as a group they provided a distraction through what seemed an interminable twilight. While she waited, she cast a dim light spell on eight cheesecloth pouches of clubmoss spores she had lined up on the parapet, after which she levitated said pouches out to various distances and heights above the town. For the moment they showed up poorly, but she knew they would be more visible after dark. Fortunately, the air was still, so she did not have to worry about them drifting very far.

Once the sky darkened to a velvety blackness, with high clouds fortuitously blocking out the two moons and the stars, the chancellor gave Sinta a sign, and she began the program with one of Bentilan's pyrotechnic spells. Though not particularly spectacular, it was extremely loud and therefore served to alert the audience below that it was time to start looking up. A vigorous casting of multicolored sparks quickly followed. Sinta then used another of Bentilan's spells, which produced explosions in the shape of flowers, to cast two stylized rosettes far below her, just above the surface of the river, using a little rose madder to tint them red. Then she targeted four of her floating pouches with small fireballs, each in a different color. Three she hit, causing satisfyingly large secondary explosions, but one pouch she overshot, so it remained for her to pick off with another fireball later. She caused a giant blue tulip to open directly over the town square, followed by a chain of multicolored sparks over the lower gatehouse. She was beginning to feel the drain on her *korethi,* but it was not yet severe. Another of Bentilan's spells enabled her to produce pyrotechnic animals—a not entirely convincing dancing bear, a strutting cockerel, and a green lizard that looked suspiciously like Angvar—followed by more colored fireballs, rosettes, and a beautiful purple iris. The spectators on the roof gasped at the animals and applauded the iris, prompting Sinta to turn and throw a small shower of multicolored sparks above their heads. She then returned to business, conjuring a fiery rabbit, a glowing daisy, and an enormous writhing dragon that consumed rather more *korethi* than she intended. Realizing that her power was waning, she ignited the last of her pouches of clubmoss spores, and finished with a complex spell of Bentilan's own devising, which produced a giant pyrotechnic version of the Sildooric princely coat of arms, with each of its heraldic devices rendered in the correct colors. The spectators on the roof applauded again, as did those on the ground. Her presentation complete, Sinta found herself sitting down, rather suddenly, on the parapet, physically and emotionally exhausted.

"Congratulations! That was most satisfactory," the chancellor told her. "Not perhaps up to Bentilan at his best, but very impressive for a debut effort. I particularly liked the crested lizard—very lifelike."

Sinta smiled weakly. "Thank you. I'm afraid the effort has left me a bit faint." When she had recovered slightly (the falconer having given her a sip of something potent from a flask he was carrying), she accompanied the chancellor back downstairs to his office. There, he directed his clerk to pay her the one hundred gold princely crowns they had agreed upon, plus five more for a job well done. Tired though she was, Sinta reflexively calculated that 105

Sildooric princely crowns were equal to about 84 Fendoric ones and roughly 101 Hrissic gold pendragons.

The chancellor thanked her again for her efforts. “I should warn you, though,” he said. “Over the last few days, I have been hearing unpleasant rumors about you. I do not trade in rumors but in established facts. Still, you should be aware that what’s being said about you is quite unflattering, both personally and professionally.”

That night Sinta dreamt yet again about the two wolves. This time she urged them emphatically to leave her alone, but they responded only with looks of wolfish disdain. When she persisted, the gray one stuck out its neck and gave a ferocious snarl that frightened her into waking up.

11

Recent discoveries of bone and fiber have led scientists to conclude that trolls, far from being mythical, inhabited the Saalic Mountains as recently as six hundred years ago.

—*The Encyclopædia Ondiricana* (12th ed.)

"I have waited for vengeance long enough," exclaimed the robed man, as he strode angrily about the gloomy underground chamber, tugging at his gray beard. "My nephew was cruelly, publicly, and shamefully executed because of that wretched girl's meddling." He pointed a bony finger at his younger companion, a pale man with a gaunt face, who looked nonplussed. "Do you have any idea how hideous was that execution? *Twenty-six* crushing blows with a wagon wheel, shattering limb after limb, bone after bone, without mercy, notwithstanding the sweet boy's gentle birth, until—hours later, mounted on the wheel, and raised to the sky for scavengers to feed on—he finally gave up the ghost. All for some worthless miller and his whore of a wife!"

The gaunt man waited for this bilious torrent to expend itself. "And what does this have to do with me?" he asked.

The robed man snorted. "You have a bitter grievance, do you not, against the sorceress Valdira? Would it not gratify you to cause her pain by helping engineer the brutal destruction of her prize pupil?"

The gaunt man allowed that it would. "Besides," he pointed out, "that prize pupil stole my pet lizard!"

"Bah!" thundered the robed man. "Speak to me not of lizards, but of blood, death, and reanimation. I want that whelp's mangled corpse to linger on in undeath, longing for the *coup de grâce* that never comes, until finally her flesh rots away and her dry bones collapse in a heap of osseous debris." He glared at the gaunt man. "You are a necromancer, are you not? Is this not within your morbid field of professional competence? Then let us scheme together. Let us lay our plans to bring down upon this common shopkeeper's brat the ignominious demise she so richly deserves!"

Unaware of the shadowy forces mobilizing against her, Sinta faced the autumn with far greater equanimity than she had the spring. Her financial situation was much more secure, and no matter what ugly slanders might be circulating about her, the unprecedented number of gold coins in her enchanted purse would surely buy her ample time to build a solid reputation in Talindor, based on her own merits.

Knowing that another 120 gold pendragons awaited her in Sirigot, once Virt completed the meticulous task of piecing together and riveting thousands of iron rings, she was not surprised, returning from an errand one afternoon, to find Othir in the kitchen. He looked, if anything, more handsome than ever, as he sweet-talked pastries out of Ferga. The circumstances, however, were not what Sinta expected.

"I believe the hauberk is almost ready at last," he told her upstairs in her study, "but that's not why I'm here. Alas, I am no longer in Lord Pirendor's service." He paused, finding it difficult, for once, to express himself. "Shortly after my investiture as a knight, I was detected in, let us say, an indiscretion—a private matter that had no conceivable bearing upon my loyalty to his lordship, or my reliability as a retainer, or my courage as a fighting man—but one which nevertheless so offended him that he abruptly dispensed with my services."

Sinta expressed her sincere condolences. She was tactful enough not to inquire after the apparently scandalous circumstances. "But, if you haven't come to fetch me to Sirigot," she asked, "why are you here in Talindor? That's a long way to travel."

Othir cleared his throat. "Yes, well, I now find myself without employment. Not wishing to resort to banditry (at least not in the near term), I seek more immediately appealing alternatives. I recalled that when you were telling me about your time as an apprentice, you mentioned that Lady Valdira employed men-at-arms, and it occurred to me that you might wish to emulate your former mistress in this regard."

Sinta considered the idea. It was not without merit. Travel would certainly be more convenient with a sturdy (not to mention entertaining) male companion. And she had a shrewd enough idea regarding the nature of Othir's "indiscretion" that she was not unduly concerned about the need to fend off his amorous advances. "Are you sure about this?" she asked. "You are now a knight. Lady Valdira is the daughter of a baron. I am the daughter of a lowly apothecary."

Othir considered this. "If you were the daughter of a savage mountain troll," he conceded, "that might be a problem, but so long as your lineage is fully human, I fail to see any insuperable obstacle."

Sinta laughed. "I think I can assure you I have no troll blood going back at least four generations."

"Then I am at your service."

Borrowing the rather uncomfortable bed from the attic, Othir moved into the smaller of the two former lumber rooms. If the other members of the household had any reservations about Sinta's bringing in the newcomer, they kept quiet about them. Ferga, whom he had already won over, began to do more fancy baking, while Ghisende became much less suspicious of Sinta, now that someone more glamorous than a master apothecary had entered the sorceress's orbit. For his part, Pentigor was too busy enthusing over the particularly rare herbs he was discovering in the pigeonholes closest to the ceiling to worry about a new fellow tenant two floors above.

No more than a week passed, in any case, before a message arrived, summoning Sinta back to Sirigot. She conferred with Othir, who assured her of his intention to accompany her there. Lord Pirendor need not know of their arrangement, he pointed out. Indeed, he need not even know that Othir had returned. This matter being settled, they turned to the question of transportation. Sinta was surprised to learn that Othir favored traveling overland.

"That's how I came here," he explained. "If you take the most direct route, it will require ten days. That's a little longer than by boat, but not much."

Happy for an excuse not to make another ocean voyage, Sinta readily agreed, and they began to make preparations for the journey. She realized how much foresight Valdira had shown in always keeping ample supplies of such foodstuffs as hardtack, cheese, and dried meat in readiness for unexpected travel. Even now that her apprenticeship was over, there were still things for her to learn from her old mentor.

What with one thing or another, they needed four days before setting out. Riding south on Tamirandalia and Othir's courser, Serifol, they passed through both the County of Menfir and the Duchy of Gol in the first three days, without any untoward incidents. Tamirandalia did pick up a stone just outside the ducal seat of Goltin, but Othir proved his usefulness by producing a hoof pick and extracting the sharp pebble that had wedged itself painfully between the horseshoe and that part of the hoof known as the frog.

Midway through the fifth day they reached the hills that marked the eastern extremity of the Saalic Mountain range. “Getting over them is about a day’s march,” Othir said. “There’s an old castle ruin that will provide us with good shelter for the night, but we must push hard to reach it before dark. They say this is troll country. I don’t know about you, but I would prefer not to meet any.”

Sinta shuddered at the thought. Though Ondiric folk tales and legends were populated with many fantastic creatures that did not actually exist, trolls were the exception, having been created many generations earlier by some magical mishap (most authorities blamed witches). The hideous misbegotten creatures lurked in the mountains and forests of the Continent, posing a menace to almost anything that moved, from squirrels to mountain goats to unwary travelers. Little was known definitively regarding their habits, but they were reported to like cold and damp, to fear fire, and to roam chiefly by twilight.

Sinta and Othir followed the road into the hills, urging Tamirandalia and Serifol to make haste, but twilight came before they reached the ruined castle. The road was poor through the hills, and Sinta was starting to wonder if they should have traveled by boat after all, when suddenly both horses reared, startled by a large troll with two heads that was blocking their path. Othir quickly regained control of Serifol and drew his sword, but Sinta nearly lost her seat and was not immediately able to do more than struggle to stay in the saddle.

“Give us gold, and we may decide not to kill you!” announced the troll’s first head, which was particularly ugly, with large bloodshot eyes, a flat snout, and a mouthful of crooked yellow teeth.

"Gold or silver," corrected the second head, which was scarcely more attractive, with a four-inch nose and many warts. "Silver is also good."

"Gold is better," insisted the first head irritably.

"We have neither gold nor silver," protested Othir smoothly, "for they are no longer valued in the distant kingdom from which we hail. But I do have several coins of the purest tin, which is now all the rage among men of quality. I shall willingly surrender them to you in exchange for our lives."

"Tin!" exclaimed the first head, its eyes bulging. "What nonsense is this?"

"Fashions change," suggested the second head. "Perhaps this man speaks the truth, and tin is now employed as a primary means of exchange."

"He does, and it is," interjected Sinta, who had regained control of Tamirandalia. "Why else would they mine it in the south of Fendoran and mint coins from it?" She touched the side of her nose. "I, too, have a valuable tin piece. Please take it, and let us pass unmolested."

Evidently trolls were immune to human charm spells, as the first head was having none of this. "What utter bosh!" it declared. "We want gold!"

"Or silver," reiterated the second head.

"Or tin," insisted Othir, undiscouraged.

"Rubbish!" screamed the first head. Enraged, it lifted an enormous fist.

Sinta judged that the troll was too close to risk attacking it with a fireball. Even if well-contained, the explosion would certainly terrify the horses. Instead, in the hope of distracting the monster from braining Serifol, who was in easiest reach, she softly uttered the incantation for the same heat spell she had used against Guild Master Tilven. (For his part, Othir urged his horse to retreat a step or two—which Serifol gladly did.) Although the troll's skin—a mottled yellow-green—did not turn red, as Tilven's had done, nor did the creature begin to sweat, both heads let out roars of pain and fury. Having asked herself what Valdira would do in this situation, Sinta canceled the spell. "Enough!" she shouted. "You are dealing with a powerful sorceress here, who tires of your trollish stupidity. We have offered you valuable tin in good faith, yet you scorn it." She conjured a tiny fireball and sent it whizzing around the troll's heads, sizzling and crackling and emitting a blistering heat. The troll foolishly swatted at it, but (luckily for everyone) missed. Sinta hastily redirected it upward, far above their heads, and detonated it in a suitably impressive explosion. "You felt the heat I can bring to bear upon your foul, moss-encrusted bodies. You saw the fire I can bring forth without flint or tinder. Now stand aside before I boil the blood in your veins and char the flesh off your misshapen bones." She conjured another fireball, which she held, hovering, in the air before her. "Do not make me use this!"

Intimidating a troll is not a task for the fainthearted, and Sinta had some trouble delivering her harangue in a suitably commanding voice, but it had the desired effect, all the same. The troll reluctantly stomped off, its heads exchanging angry recriminations, as they litigated which one was to blame for this embarrassing retreat.

Othir cackled with glee. "Now *that's* how to handle a troll!"

Sinta extinguished her unexploded fireball with a gesture. "Even so, let's get out of here, before it changes its minds and comes back to pound us into a sticky paste."

12

As early as his apprenticeship, the wizard Togrod had distinguished himself by devising a dramatically more efficient approach to transfiguration. He went on to serve as the king's magician through no fewer than three reigns, producing numerous magical innovations, including many for use on the battlefield (albeit at the behest of his sovereigns rather than by his own inclination).

—*The Secret History of Esdiric Wizardry*

"What progress, necromancer?" demanded the robed man with the irritability typical of him. It was three weeks since their initial meeting.

"Our preparations are complete," replied the gaunt man, who now had a large raven on his shoulder. "The bait has been most cunningly contrived and a suitable hook has been procured upon which to dangle it."

"And the girl?" The robed man produced a wand from his pocket and twirled it between his fingers. "What of the girl, necromancer?"

The gaunt man stroked the raven's shiny blue-black feathers. "Corvin here has just returned from Sirigot to report her arrival last night, haven't you, my sweet?" (The raven gave a gurgling croak in confirmation.) "Our agent is in place and awaits only your final order to proceed."

"Then let him have it," declared the robed man fiercely. "Damn it all—it's time for us to spring our trap!"

❦

Sinta had indeed arrived in Sirigot, without further adventures of note along the way, although once south of the mountains, she enjoyed the opportunity to see more of the Duchy of Hriss. Comparing the ways the Ondiric and Esdiric cultures had blended with the ways they had stayed resolutely separate was fascinating to her. The food was also extremely tasty, in part because cooks could avail themselves of a wider variety of fresh ingredients in Hriss than they could further north.

Having no wish to dream about wolves again, Sinta stretched the final enchantments to Lord Pirendor's armor over two days, rather than completing them more exhaustingly in one. Virt had done a superb job of piecing the mail together into a hauberk that fit Lord Pirendor well, and Sinta's enchantments gave it reduced weight, increased flexibility, and much surer protection. Delighted, the baron was free with his praise of both Virt and Sinta—though he stopped short of topping off his third and final payment to Sinta with any sort of bonus.

Othir made himself scarce the entire time. Sinta thought it might seem odd, however, if she did not inquire after him with Lord Pirendor, so the first night at supper she asked, as innocently as possible, why he was not present. Such a good-looking boy! Had he not been about to complete his training and become a knight? The baroness turned pale at the mere mention of his name, and the baron muttered something about promising young men who proved to be bitter disappointments. Doing her best to avoid awkward conversational topics for the remainder of her visit, Sinta had a pleasant stay, though in truth she had little in common with her hosts, the baroness in particular.

⸙

On Sinta's final evening in Sirigot, a peddler presented himself at the castle. He was a strange-looking man, not in his first youth, with weirdly compelling eyes but an untrustworthy mouth. Normally such a person would have been turned away at the gate, but this man was liberal with his silver griffins, and in one instance whispered a few words in the wizarding tongue that resulted in his interlocutor's skeptical treatment of him simply melting away. Once admitted, he ingratiated himself to the baron by selling him some handsome pieces of jewelry for a fraction of their true worth.

"I have heard tell that you have a sorceress staying with you," the peddler remarked, as he packed up his wares to leave.

The baron conceded that this was true.

"I have something that might interest such a person," the peddler continued. "I don't pretend to understand magical matters myself, but I know sorcerer script when I see it, so if nothing else I would value an expert's opinion."

The promised "something" proved to be a sheet of battered vellum, covered with magical writing in a minute hand. Wary that it might contain a curse of some kind, Sinta examined it cautiously but found that it held instead a clever bit of sorcery designed to render the spell caster immune to snake and spider venoms. Accompanying the spell was an extensive learned commentary. Intriguingly, the manuscript was in fact a palimpsest, with washed out wizard script barely legible beneath the sorcery. This wizard script did not itself appear to be a spell, but rather something discursive regarding a famous Esdiric wizard named Togrod. Sinta was indeed interested, and since the peddler claimed not to know precisely what the manuscript was, he asked a reasonable price to begin with and allowed himself to be bargained down to an even more favorable one.

Sinta stayed up late that night, first reading the commentary on the spell to counteract venom, which she found interesting though not profound, then puzzling her way through the wizarding discourse, which was extremely difficult to make out, bordering in places on the illegible. Of course, she enjoyed the challenge, but she also found the content engaging in its own right. She had heard of Togrod and knew him to have been a wizard of wide-ranging interests and great inventiveness. The text, which purported to be a personal memorial by someone who had known him well, confirmed all of this, and claimed, tantalizingly, that Togrod had insisted that his entire library be interred, in secret, along with him in the great Esdiric necropolis of Chilchenteros.

"Change of plan," she told Othir the next morning, when they met up to begin their return journey. "We're going to Esdiron."

The gaunt man had been right: the peddler's manuscript *was* cunningly contrived, both to escape detection as a forgery (the spell, for example, was genuine) and to pique Sinta's native curiosity. In the normal course of things, she disapproved of people raiding tombs, but here the temptation was too great. Her unseen enemies had succeeded in turning her unquenchable thirst for knowledge—surely one of her defining strengths—into a weakness they could exploit against her.

13

Lentiran, in western Hriss, was largely destroyed in the most recent Esdiro-Ondiric war. It has since been rebuilt in the most modern style, funded by the reparations imposed upon Esdiron in the peace settlement. The steel-and-glass civic center is of particular note, as is the new university complex.

— *Hriss on 10 Crowns a Day*

Four straight days of cold drizzle did not get the journey off to a propitious start. The horses firmly disapproved and longed for a warm, dry stable, but they had no vote. Sinta and Othir could not be said to have enjoyed the rain, either, but they persevered. On the fifth day the weather cleared, and Sinta began to note the increasing Esdiric cultural influence as they approached the border. Especially prominent were the temples of the Tiralist sect, with their brightly colored domes and festive cemeteries. When the travelers arrived in the town of Lentiran late that afternoon, Sinta also heard more people speaking Esdiric on the street.

While they were looking for a suitable inn at which to spend the night, Sinta noticed a shop advertised by a single character from the sorcerers' syllabary, unexpectedly joined, with a calligraphic flourish, to a letter from the wizarding alphabet. Both characters, standing alone, were traditionally used as symbols for the concept of esoterica. Sinta asked Othir to look after the horses, while she went inside to investigate.

The tiny shop was empty but for a rather attractive young shopkeeper, his large gray cat, and a bare counter. This minimalist approach to merchandizing stood in stark contrast to Sinta's experience with other such shops, which were usually cluttered from floor to ceiling with worthless junk purporting to have some unlikely magical power or other.

Sinta greeted the shopkeeper first in the mystical language of sorcery, then again in that of wizardry. Neither tongue was well suited—or often used—for conversation, but both featured conventional greetings that were preferable, from Sinta's point of view, to secret handshakes, or some such.

The shopkeeper returned the conventional response in both languages, along with a surprised but beautiful smile. Not wishing to be left out, the cat rubbed itself against the visitor's legs. While Sinta was not afraid of cats, she did not trust them. In her experience, they always had an agenda. Nevertheless, she reached down and scratched this one behind the ears, eliciting a throaty purr.

"He likes you," said the shopkeeper in Ondiric. "That's unusual."

"He is a handsome beast," Sinta conceded. She looked around the seemingly empty shop. "Forgive me, but you do not appear to be overstocked."

The shopkeeper smiled. "We prioritize quality over quantity." With a wave of his hand, seven objects appeared on the counter. He picked up a velvet-lined case holding an exquisite piece of gold jewelry. "To begin with the best, this necklace will protect the woman who wears it from any and all hostile spells, no matter how powerful."

Sinta raised her eyebrows. "Nice! And if a man were to wear it?"

The shopkeeper grimaced. "Quite apart from arousing suspicions of effeminacy, it would have the opposite effect of making him *more* vulnerable to such spells." He ran a finger over the fine filigree. "You can see from the workmanship that it's a very old piece. That it remains effective gives me confidence that its protective force is undiminishing, unlike most devices of like conception that can only absorb a limited amount of magical power before they burn out. I suspect the underlying principle is that it actually uses the magical power directed against it to recharge itself."

Sinta acknowledged that it was a fine item. "I assume it also carries a fine price?"

The shopkeeper nodded. "You assume correctly. Six thousand gold pendragons."

Sinta gave a low whistle. It was more money than she had received for her father's business. "Regrettably, that is more than I can afford."

The shopkeeper closed the case and picked up a brass inkwell instead. "This clever bit of enchantment will no doubt suit your budget better. It may not look like much, but it remains ever full, never running out of ink or drying up. Furthermore, it has a useful safety feature." He turned it upside down. No ink spilled out. "If you tip it over, there is no danger it will ruin your work or stain your desk, let alone fill your home and hearth with an endless sea of ink, should the tipping be done in your absence by, say, a negligent feline."

The shopkeeper's cat mewed, evidently recognizing that some sort of aspersion had been directed its way.

Sinta laughed. "Very nice! Yes, I could be tempted by such an item, if the price were right. How much are you asking?"

The shopkeeper gave her another winning smile. "Just ten pendragons." He held up a warning finger. "Non-negotiable. I find haggling exceptionally tedious."

Sinta nodded. "I'll think about it. Now, what are these other treasures?"

The shopkeeper held up a nondescript ring. "Adorning a finger, this odd little item does nothing at all. Adorning a toe, however, it allows the wearer to eat all manner of ill-advised food without suffering from indigestion. At your time of life, you probably have no need for such a thing, but perhaps you have a middle-aged or elderly relative who is not so fortunate?"

Sinta shook her head. "No, I may live to regret the decision someday, but unusual though the item is, I will decline to purchase it today."

Unfazed, the shopkeeper pointed to a stoppered flask. "Here we have a potion that lets the drinker breathe underwater for up to an hour. I know for certain that's what it does, because I brewed it myself. I'll admit it tastes dreadful, but that scarcely diminishes its usefulness."

Sinta considered whether such a potion might not be a good thing to have with her the next time she was obliged to take an ocean voyage, but the fact that she did not know how to swim seemed to limit its practical value. "And these dice?" she asked. "What is their enchantment?"

The shopkeeper had the grace to look embarrassed. "Ah, yes, I'm hoping you are not the sort of person who would have a use for those. They are enchanted to throw whatever combination you desire." He demonstrated, calling out each throw in advance. "Four. Seven. Snake-eyes. Ten. A dishonest gambler's dream, especially since he can deliberately lose as often as necessary to avoid detection."

Sinta shook her head. "No, they are not for me, but you should be sure to charge whoever buys them a ridiculous sum."

The shopkeeper grinned. "Oh, I will!" He moved on to a small volume, bound in snakeskin. "I am given to understand that this is an introductory guide to the practice of witchcraft, but since I can't read it, I can't offer any guarantee. It contains a few lurid illustrations that seem consistent with its being such a work, but for all I know it could just be a collection of rather niche pornography. So, if genuine: extremely rare, most valuable; but unauthenticated, without my personal guarantee: heavily discounted, forty pendragons."

Sinta examined the manuscript inside the snakeskin covers with great interest. It was written in a script she had never seen before. The ink drawings did appear to relate to witchcraft—whether they depicted someone calling down a hailstorm or summoning an incubus. Hoping, as she did, one day to untangle some of the mysteries surrounding this highly secretive magical tradition, she was much tempted. "And what about this other volume?" she asked, pointing to the much larger tome resting on the counter next to it.

The shopkeeper opened its cheap covers and removed a loose sheet of parchment. "We have here a wizard's working spell book. Based on the contents, I would judge it to date from toward the end of his apprenticeship." He handed her the loose sheet. "I've prepared a list of its contents. As you can see, it contains some interesting things."

Sinta examined the list with care. Many of the spells she already had, but the shopkeeper was right that some more unusual items were also present. There was, for example, a spell to neutralize poison in food and drink. Another claimed to impart the extraordinary eyesight of an eagle. But the one that particularly drew Sinta's attention severed the control a necromancer exercised over the corpses and skeletons that he (or, less often, she) had reanimated, for as Sinta understood it, the undead resented their reanimation and would turn on the person responsible, if only they could.

"Hmm," she said, feigning a casual lack of interest, "I suppose spell books like this must come on the market fairly frequently, as older magicians die off." She turned her attention to the manuscript itself. "Goodness, what appalling handwriting! How unfortunate. One would have to be extraordinarily careful not to misread a spell from it, given the potentially dangerous results."

The shopkeeper made a conciliatory gesture. "You are, of course, correct on both counts, as the modest price of just eighty pendragons duly reflects."

Now apprised of all the available merchandise, Sinta requested a quill to test whether the inkwell actually worked. She also examined the two bound manuscripts more carefully. The shopkeeper's prices were high, she decided, but not exorbitant, and as a shopkeeper's daughter, she recognized both that he must have significant overhead and that he was not making his profit on volume. "I'll take these three," she said at last, indicating the inkwell and the two manuscripts.

"Excellent," said the shopkeeper. "That totals 130 gold pendragons—but because Fenthengir likes you" (he gave her that smile again), "I'll accept 125." Hearing his name, Fenthengir resumed bumping his furry head against Sinta's ankles.

While the shopkeeper prepared a receipt using the magic inkwell, Sinta got out her enchanted money purse, backed away from the counter for privacy, and whispered the password *monstrous lizard* to access its extradimensional pocket. She then returned to the counter and counted out the requisite pendragons in twenty-five neat stacks of five.

"A nice piece of work, that," the shopkeeper remarked, indicating the purse. He selected two stacks of pendragons at random and examined the coins for authenticity. "Very good." With a wave of his hand, all 125 pendragons disappeared, along with the necklace, ring, flask, and dice. He handed over her purchases and receipt. "A pleasure doing business with you, miss. Please come again!"

14

Legroshen of Grook, Third Count of Denchog. Son of Shentek, the Second Count, and Lady Kantel. Remembered for his fanatical interest in blood sports. Died without issue along with his wife, Lady Tilgel, during the second peasant uprising of the reign of Choofren III, thus extinguishing the line.

—*A Genealogical Guide to the Noble Houses of Esdiron*

On the sixth day, Sinta and Othir crossed the River Vilta into Esdiron. The Ondiric town of Casirn stood on the left bank, the Esdiric town of Kasesh-i-Viltech on the right, with just one bridge between them. Sinta had never experienced a border-crossing like it. So far as she knew, only merchants were ever inspected for possible import duties on their goods. The Esdir, however, inspected everyone crossing the bridge, and they had the most extraordinary ideas of what should be subject to duty. Operating according to a posted schedule of hundreds of dutiable goods, covering most of the exterior wall of the customs house, the Esdiric officials informed the travelers that horses, saddles, armor, weapons, writings in magical scripts, fruits (Sinta had bought a bag of apples in Casirn), brass inkwells, and live lizards were all subject to duty, totaling, in their case, 1 gold *troog*, 9 silver *poog*, and 3 copper *tesh*. Since Sinta had no Esdiric currency, the officials applied a highly unfavorable rate of exchange to demand instead 2 gold wyverns and 6 silver griffins. She was sorely tempted to try charming them but decided the risk of detection and punishment was too high. She sought relief instead—unusually for her—in profanity, expressing herself under her breath in Tseren, as the Esdir were less likely to understand it. When the customs official who finally gave them permission to pass actually had the gall to say, "Welcome to Esdiron," it was all Sinta could do not to throw a heat spell on him.

Othir was somewhat disconcerted by this previously unsuspected side of his employer's personality, and he did his best to calm her down by suggesting that they spend the rest of the day looking around Kasesh-i-Viltech. He had been to the town before, so he knew some of the more interesting things to see. Accordingly, they visited a four-hundred-year-old Asardian temple that was a masterpiece of late Rendiric architecture. They also saw a recently completed Chingezian *toorif,* where members of that cult honored their ancestors with burnt offerings. A stop at the central market gave Sinta an opportunity to practice her Esdiric. She replenished her supply of grubs for Angvar and bought some exotic imported citrus fruit for herself and Othir. Some unintended hilarity ensued when she asked an old woman selling *tranesh* (fruit pastries) for two *dranesh* (sandgrouse). Othir, whose Esdiric was very good, laughed so hard his horse worried that he might be ill, while the old woman was so tickled she wanted to give

Sinta the pastries for free. Sinta, however, rather stiffly insisted on paying for them. She also gave Othir a poke with her quarterstaff to let him know that his employer did not think her mistake was *that* funny.

⚜

In the evenings Sinta studied her new spell book, struggling to accustom herself to the execrable handwriting of its compiler. What she would have preferred to do was cleanly re-copy the new spells, but the inns at which she and Othir stayed did not provide such amenities as tables or desks, and she had not brought along a sufficient supply of blank parchment in any case, so she felt effectively thwarted until she could return home.

⚜

The Esdiric countryside was not dramatically different from that of Hriss, at least along the route west from the border to the capital city of Feldross. It was highly agricultural, whether planted with grain, vines, or fruit trees. Sinta had the impression, however, that the peasantry was faring badly, a fact suggesting that the nobility extracted an even crueler share of the land's bounty than was the case in Ondiran.

Nor did Sinta's first encounter with an Esdiric nobleman suggest that they improved on acquaintance.

It was the morning of the second day after leaving Kasesh-i-Viltech. Sinta and Othir came to a fork in the road, with no signage indicating the way to the capital. A carriage soon approached, however, escorted by four armed horsemen and followed by a train of servants. Painted a garish shade of yellow, the carriage itself was not like anything Sinta had ever seen before: unlike the wagons with which she was familiar, it had a fully enclosed passenger compartment, suspended on chains above the vehicle's chassis for a smoother ride. An elaborate heraldic crest ornamented the door to the passenger compartment. As the vehicle drew up, Othir hailed its accompanying horsemen to ask the way.

He received no civil reply, the lead horseman demanding instead just who he thought he was to interrupt the journey of the Count and Countess of Denchog. Taking offense, Othir replied with some heat that he was a knight of the Ondiric Empire, but even had he been a wandering minstrel he would surely have been due a more courteous reception.

At this point a balding man with a goatee stuck his head out of the carriage and demanded an explanation for the delay.

"Just some stupid Ondir, my lord, who doesn't even know the way to the capital," the lead horseman called back to him.

"This is outrageous!" cried the count. "Tell him to remove himself from the roadway, along with that shabbily dressed concubine of his, so that her ladyship and I may continue on our way unmolested by foreign riffraff."

Othir's courtly training had inculcated in him perhaps too deeply the importance of defending his personal honor—not to mention that of any female companion—

without due regard for the likely consequences. He therefore expressed the view that the count was a common cur, a mongrel in the guise of higher nobility, who should be beaten with a stick until he learned to comport himself with the humility befitting his base canine nature.

Sinta did not like the direction in which this encounter seemed to be headed, even if a few of the choicer insults, such as "concubine" and "mongrel" had exceeded the limits of her Esdiric vocabulary.

Apoplectic with rage at Othir's critique of his ancestral line, the count ordered his horsemen to "teach the insolent puppy and his whore a lesson" in the behavior proper to "foreign scum" while on Esdiric soil.

The horsemen, correctly interpreting this educational mandate as metaphor, drew their swords and spurred their mounts into action. Well trained, they quickly separated so as to bring home their attack from different directions. As a result, Sinta lost her chance to throw a spell affecting all of them together.

Othir parried the lead horseman's first blow but was unable to avoid a slashing attack by the second man. His armor held, but he still grunted in pain at the force of the impact. Even as he did so, however, he succeeded in driving the point of his own sword into the left armpit of his attacker. The mail links gave way, and the second horseman gave an agonized shout as Othir pressed the thrust home. There was a great effusion of blood, and the unfortunate man had to drop his sword in order to clamp a hand over the wound in a desperate attempt to staunch the bleeding.

Sinta, meanwhile, had troubles enough of her own, as the other two horsemen bore down upon her from opposite sides. Being slightly farther away, she had a little more time to react, but not being a skilled horsewoman, she was having difficulty controlling Tamirandalia, who—never having had the slightest pretensions to being a warhorse—was close to panic. Nevertheless, Sinta managed to cast a spell known as the "magician's fist" at the foremost rider before he reached her. It was the same spell that had underlain the protective wards she had cast on her moving crates, and it conjured an invisible fist that caught the man full in the chest, forcibly enough, given the collision with his own forward momentum, to unseat him. Sinta then permitted the terrified rouncey to obey her instinct to flee, closely pursued by the fourth horseman.

Othir remained in combat with the leader of the four men. Serifol did his part, delivering a vicious bite to the other horse, which screamed and tried to withdraw, only to be forcibly restrained by its rider. This distraction enabled Othir to deal a blow to the horseman's thigh, but nothing decisive. The second horseman, meanwhile, was well on his way to bleeding to death from a severed artery. He had managed to dismount but was staggering around helplessly, fast growing faint from loss of blood.

Sinta turned in the saddle at a full gallop and cast a heat spell but missed the fourth horseman by a wide margin. She swore, in Ondiric this time, and urged Tamirandalia on. She had no desire to harm her pursuer's horse, but she needed an area spell that required no great accuracy in targeting. Accordingly she tossed a fireball behind her, detonating it almost immediately. She could feel the heat on her back as it exploded. Both the horseman and his mount gave cries of distress and broke off pursuit. She had tried to calibrate her casting so as to avoid killing either of them, but both suffered painful burns.

Sinta circled back to the continuing battle at the fork. On the way she used her quarterstaff to concuss the third horseman, who had gotten up and was attempting to retrieve his mount. Othir was still holding his own, but the fight was well matched. Sinta intervened by charming his opponent's horse, which suddenly began to buck, attempting to throw and then trample its rider. Othir and Serifol pulled back and allowed the animal to carry out this agenda unhindered.

Her side having prevailed, Sinta dismounted to see if there was anything she could do for the second horseman, now lying unconscious on the ground, but he was beyond saving. "Damnation!" she shouted at Othir. "I did not hire you to get us into unnecessary death matches with the retinues of highborn noblemen." Turning to the carriage, she addressed herself to the count, who had watched the defeat of his four retainers with growing dismay: "That said, he wasn't wrong—your lordship richly deserves to be beaten like a dog." Instead of doing that, however, she put the now cowering nobleman into a deep sleep. One after another, the countess, the servants, and those horsemen who were still conscious, as well as the horse she had hit with the fireball, followed him into magical slumber. She turned back to Othir. "There will be no end of trouble if any of them remembers what happened here. After all, you've killed a man—or mortally wounded him anyway. Nor did the count seem like a fair-minded, forgiving fellow." She pointed at the badly scorched but now sleeping horse. "And since this whole mess is to no small degree your fault, Othir, you're the one who's going to have to put that poor beast down."

Othir looked duly remorseful and chose, for once, to remain silent.

Sinta began the laborious process of throwing spells to induce permanent short-term memory loss on the count and each person in his retinue. Ironically, she always had difficulty remembering how to cast this particular spell, and she did not have the requisite spell book along, so she had to use a special remembering spell to recall the forgotten incantation. "Now let us be gone before anyone wakes up," she told Othir upon finishing. "It's a pity we still don't know which road leads to the capital."

15

Feldross is the metropolitan heart of Esdiron's vibrant cultural life. It is accordingly packed with museums, monuments, and important architecture. We recommend at least three days to see the major sights, but most visitors will want to stay at least a week to experience the vibrant life of the city itself. Resentment of the Ondir lingers, however, particularly in the older generation.

—Esdiron on 12 Crowns a Day

With over 100,000 inhabitants, Feldross was bigger by far than any city in Ondiran or Tserenets. Located at the confluence of three rivers, it had at its core the royal palace, built on a small but heavily fortified island. The city walls formed concentric circles, twice built anew as the city outgrew the old ones, though the latest were already being outstripped again by new construction, as indentured workers, prisoners, and slaves drained the swampland to the south. It was an exciting city of commerce and culture, the site of multiple markets, the Continent's first university, and the monasteries of three competing religions, but it was also a dismal city of filth and disease, of poverty and crime, a dangerous, unhealthful place, where the death rate far exceeded the birthrate, so that its growth depended on a steady influx of migrants from the countryside. Nevertheless it was a place where a determined populace seemed finally to have surmounted centuries of stagnation. Sinta had never seen or imagined anything like it. Chilchenteros, she decided, could wait a few days, while they explored Feldross.

And there was much to interest her, from the intricate astronomical clock outside the city hall, to the covered sewer under construction in one of the wealthier districts. On a single street she found the shops of no fewer than four competing apothecaries and two alchemists, and on another, three different freelance wizards had hung out their shingles. There were weird religious processions in the streets, as well as armies of beggars, street performers, and prostitutes. Everywhere jostling, noise, stench, and the Esdiric penchant for bright colors assailed the senses. It was, Sinta soon concluded, both exhilarating and overwhelming.

Unfortunately, it became somewhat more overwhelming on the second day of their visit. After Othir teasingly averred that an elegant velvet hat on display in one of the city's many markets would make people less likely to mistake Sinta for his shabbily dressed concubine, she tried to buy it, only to discover that someone had stolen her enchanted coin purse.

Knowing the risk of pickpockets and cutpurses, Sinta had of course taken precautions against them. One was the design of the purse itself. No thief would realize it had a second, extradimensional compartment, and even if someone did, without the magic password they had no way of gaining access to it. To be sure, this precaution was only useful if the rightful owner could recover the purse. To do that, Sinta had enchanted it with a sophisticated locater spell—the invention of her mentor, Valdira, who had once used it to rescue Sinta herself after she had been magically abducted.

"Someone has stolen my coin purse," she told Othir. "If we can duck into that archway over there, I'll cast a spell to find it." First she threw a simple summoning spell, just in case the purse was still within range. Unsurprisingly, it was not. Then she closed her eyes and cast Valdira's locater spell. She turned sharply to the left. "It's in this direction!" she told Othir, pointing, her eyes still tightly closed. I can see that it's indoors now, in a sort of old warehouse. I think the thief must have just turned it over to the man he works for. It's lying empty on a pile of other empty purses, while the thief receives his share, and his boss puts the rest of the money in an iron strongbox. Or perhaps that's a different thief, who's arrived after ours. No matter. I don't care about him. It's the purse I want." She gesticulated with her fingers. "Pulling back, I've got a view now of the building they're in, and pulling back further, of the street. Very seedy. Not a nice part of town." She opened her eyes. "All right, let's go. That purse has most of my savings in it, and that means your wages, as well!"

The crooked streets and alleyways of the old city made it difficult to follow the beeline revealed by Sinta's spell, forcing her to recast it several times.

"I wouldn't go in there," warned an unkempt man leading a ferret on a string, as they turned a corner and started down a particularly narrow street. "That's Thieves' Town, that is. The cutthroats in there don't take kindly to strangers."

"Thanks for the warning," Sinta replied, "but they have something of mine." Nevertheless, she could not help feeling nervous. When the unkempt man shrugged and continued on his way, she called out to him. "What do you know about a tall man with short black hair and a picture of a—what do you call it in Esdiric?—a turtle, breathing fire, on the back of his left hand?"

The man turned. "That's Choss, the king of Thieves' Town," he replied. "They say he's also a wizard, or was one once. You don't want to mess with him!"

"Better and better," sighed the sorceress in Ondiric.

They were now close enough for the locater spell to yield a more readily navigable path to their destination. Sinta had just remarked that it felt like they were being watched, when someone emptied a chamber pot, without warning, onto the street from a window two floors above, barely missing them. Cautiously they emerged onto the main thoroughfare of Thieves' Town, where various shady characters were scuttling furtively about. Othir unsheathed his sword. "I feel very conspicuous here," he remarked. "Like a corpse at a wedding, or a bride at a funeral."

Outside Choss's headquarters, two imposing thugs stood guard with long wrought-iron rods in their grip. Sinta could feel her nervousness rising.

"We're here to see Choss," Othir announced loudly.

"Beat it, pretty boy!" said the first thug.

"Yeah, get lost, nightie-knight," sneered the second. "The girlie can stay, though."

Sinta gestured wordlessly, and the first thug yawned, slumped back against the wall, and slid, snoring, to the ground. "Hey!" objected the second, just before following his colleague's example.

Grinning, Othir opened the door and stepped inside the cavernous former warehouse. Sinta followed, clutching her quarterstaff as though her life depended on it—which, to be fair, it very soon might. Choss was holding court by the far wall, attended by a pretty but poorly groomed woman dressed as a common prostitute, along with two obvious criminal lieutenants and twelve low-life toughs, four of whom were administering a brutal beating to yet another man for some minor infraction of their apparently strict code of conduct. Choss signaled for them to stop and bade them to surround their guests at the door, instead. Most were toting blunt instruments of one kind or another, though Othir wielded his sword in such a way as to keep them at a respectful distance.

Choss ran the hand with the turtle tattoo over his unshaven chin. "You're very foolish to come here, whoever you are."

Othir gave him a haughty look. "Not as foolish as you are to think so!"

Sinta cast her summoning spell. The purse lifted off and sailed toward her, but one of the toughs, with the dexterity of a practiced thief, plucked it from the air as it flew past. He then took it to Choss, who examined it with interest, casting a quick spell himself. The purse glowed for a moment.

"So, it's enchanted," he said, turning it inside out and back again. "That explains why you want it back. But what does it do?"

Sinta used the butt of her quarterstaff to fend off one of the toughs, who had inched too close for her liking. "There's a spell on it that let me follow it here."

Choss scoffed. "That doesn't seem like enough by itself to justify your risking your lives for an empty purse. Not unless you're extremely stupid."

Othir coughed. "Extreme stupidity," he submitted, "has more explanatory power in human affairs than you might suppose."

"Perhaps," Choss conceded, "but not, I think, in this case. No matter—you two will tell me what I need to know soon enough." He uttered a guttural incantation and gestured toward them with both hands.

With a gasp, Othir doubled over, as excruciating pain gripped his insides, while Sinta felt Grulfar's amulet grow warm against her skin, as it absorbed the spell power directed at her. She twirled her quarterstaff to keep the toughs at bay, even as she quickly cast a spell of her own to cancel Choss's. She had to put quite a bit of *korethi* into it to be sure it would succeed.

Othir straightened up again. He had managed not to drop his sword, but only just. "That was extremely unpleasant," he conceded, "but it gained you nothing."

"On the contrary," Choss replied, "watching you writhe like a child with colic was quite a treat."

Anger temporarily displaced Sinta's fear, and she conjured a "magician's fist" to strike Choss full in the face. To her dismay, nothing happened, for he, too, had some sort of magical protection. He had thus provoked her into wasting both crucial seconds and *korethi.* Fortunately, she still managed to throw up an invisible defensive barrier in time to block his next spell. One she had never seen before, it sent a cluster of magic darts hurtling through the air toward Othir. They struck Sinta's magical barrier instead and disintegrated in little puffs of greenish-yellow smoke.

Choss's two capos now advanced, knives in hand, to rally the twelve toughs for a frontal assault. Sinta hastily threw her blindness spell on all fourteen. To disorient and demoralize them further, she followed it up with deafness.

"Your men are helpless," Othir called out to Choss, "and so far your girlfriend hasn't been good for much, either, beyond providing some rather low-rent decoration. Your spells can't hurt the lady I serve, and now she has shielded me from them, too. It's time to surrender that purse, which you don't even know how to use. You have the money that was in it. Be content!"

Choss growled with frustration. Although he knew some effective spells, he was not, in fact, an especially powerful wizard. "I can always destroy it," he threatened. "How would you like that?"

Othir shook his head. "Oh, I definitely wouldn't recommend anything so foolish. The lady here would resent it, and you don't want to be the object of her resentment. Up to now she's shown restraint. She doesn't like to kill folk. But antagonize her, and I promise you'll find out what an angry sorceress is capable of."

This discussion gave Sinta the breathing room to cast two spells in quick succession. The first created a circle of impenetrable inky darkness around Choss's female companion, wide enough to encompass Choss, as well. Since she had not cast the spell at the wizard himself, whatever was blocking spells for him could not thwart it. For that matter, he had no way of being certain what exactly had just happened. The likeliest explanation under the circumstances seemed to be that she had somehow overcome his protection against hostile spells and blinded him, as she had just done with his men. He therefore tried to cast a spell canceling it, but since no spell had actually been cast upon him, this effort was unavailing. In the meantime, Sinta cast her summoning spell again, and the coin purse flew out of his hands and into hers.

Seizing the moment, Othir rushed across the warehouse floor, pushing aside blinded and deafened flunkies, until he reached the edge of the circle of darkness, close to where Choss had been standing. Sword in hand, he gestured urgently to Sinta to cancel the spell, but before she could do so, the terrified woman at the center of the darkness chanced to step far enough away from Choss to restore him to the light. Othir then took a single stride forward and without hesitation ran the startled wizard through. "Now *you* know what it's like to writhe like a child with colic," he whispered and wrenched his sword free from the man's viscera, having ended the reign of the King of Thieves' Town for good.

“Let’s get out of here!” shouted Sinta, but Othir stopped first to wipe his sword on Choss’s tunic. He removed a ring from the dying man’s finger and a talisman from around his neck. He also closed the iron strongbox full of coins and hefted it onto his shoulder. Only then did he follow Sinta back out into the street, where they saw that opportunistic passers-by had stripped the two sleeping thugs of their clothes and weapons.

⚜

Once they had returned to the inn where they were staying, Sinta determined that both the ring and the talisman were enchanted. A few different spells and a little experimentation established that the talisman was what provided protection against magic, while the ring enabled night vision and stealthy movement. Othir was pleased to have both, and Sinta agreed that they were his by right. She also acknowledged his claim to the strongbox and its contents, which totaled 12 gold coins of different origins and denominations, 132 silver ones, 492 copper, 31 bronze, 40 brass, 56 tin, 4 that Sinta thought were probably zinc, and 2 Tseren iron pieces (both of which had come from Sinta’s purse). As best he could figure it (with a little help from Sinta), the entire haul was worth slightly more than 13 Hrissic gold pendragons.

“It’s a pity we can’t return the money to all the people Choss’s gang of thieves stole it from,” he admitted, “but since we can’t, I promise to give it a good home.”

16

Just four miles from the capital, the necropolis of Chilchenteros has only recently been opened for tourism (admission: 1 *troog;* guided tour: 3 *troog).* Although the above-ground cemetery is of surpassing size, filled with family tombs and individual graves, some dating back more than a millennium, the catacombs are what have made the site famous. This extensive network of tunnels, lined with human bones and leading to larger galleries, chapels, and ossuaries, is a masterpiece of macabre religious sentiment of the type for which the Esdir have always been known. The road from the capital is good, though parking facilities remain rudimentary. A petrol station and a souvenir shop are located in the village nearby.

— *The Motor-Tourist's Guide to Esdiron* (1st ed.)

The raven flapped impatiently against the innkeeper's door, uttering shrill crics. It had important information. The innkeeper, who felt a superstitious dread of the carrion-feeder, reluctantly let it inside. He was being well paid not to question what the gaunt man in black had been doing each night at the necropolis, and putting up with his sinister pet, as it came and went at all hours, was a regrettable part of the bargain. Once inside, the bird flew to the gaunt man's room. The innkeeper followed and opened the door for it, before returning to his morning duties with a shudder.

The raven landed on the bed where the gaunt man was still sleeping and gave him an urgent peck on the hand, accompanied by further raucous cries. The bird had been surveilling Sinta and Othir, on and off, since their arrival in Sirigot, and now that they had quit Feldross in the direction of Chilchenteros, it had flown ahead to warn its master. They would be there soon.

⚜

It was the morning after the events in Thieves' Town. Though Sinta wanted to explore Feldross further, she was concerned about the possible repercussions of Choss's death. Chances were that no one would mourn him, that one of his lieutenants would simply take his place, but she did not feel comfortable waiting to see what the criminal underworld might or might not do to avenge the death of its leader. Besides, she was eager to find Togrod's alleged library, even if it did mean rummaging around in a necropolis, of all places.

Having reached Chilchenteros after an hour's ride, Sinta and Othir tied their horses to a hitching post outside the main gate. She cast a security spell on them out of force of habit, unlikely though it seemed that anyone at the deserted site would attempt to steal them. The place was huge, and in its way rather beautiful, with row after row of elaborate family tombs, as well as many impressive individual graves. Esdiric funerary sculpture, Sinta discovered, was an art form unto itself, of which she had no prior inkling.

The manuscript stated that Togrod's tomb was underground in the catacombs, though it did not say *where* in the catacombs it might be. They soon found the broad descending staircase that led to the large unlocked double gate that formed the entrance. Sinta cast a light spell on one end of her quarterstaff, and Othir threw open the gate, revealing parallel rows of burning votive candles that lined one particular path deeper into the complex.

"Well, that's unexpected," Sinta said after a moment's hesitation, "not to say bizarre, but I suppose we may as well start by seeing where they lead."

"And who set them up?" Othir suggested skeptically.

Sinta grimaced, preferring not to admit how nervous the prospect made her.

The walls of the tunnels were lined with centuries' worth of bones, for the Esdir had begun constructing the catacombs nearly seven hundred years earlier. The bones were arranged in decorative geometric patterns, sometimes interrupted by elaborate figurative designs, mostly depicting the religious symbols of one sect or another. The candles led fairly quickly to a doorway that opened onto a large gallery featuring some sort of stone platform or altar, ornamented with bones and set in the center of the floor beneath an elaborate chandelier made entirely of bones. There were also many more votive candles, arranged in decorative patterns near the walls, which were of course also lined with bones. A door led off in each direction.

Eerie though the place might be, Sinta's curiosity was now definitely getting the better of her. She and Othir stepped inside, whereupon the door in the far wall swung open, and the gaunt man strode in, raven on his shoulder, followed by four shambling figures, whose pallid, moist, unwholesome-looking skin appeared to be in the early stages of decomposition. With one wave of his hand, the necromancer slammed shut the door behind Sinta and Othir. With another, he threw open the doors to either side, and sixteen skeletons danced into the room.

"Hello, Sinta," he said, as the skeletons and reanimated corpses advanced. "All grown up, I see. But where is my purloined lizard, I wonder?" (Angvar was in fact outside, snug in his travel basket.)

Sinta stared at the necromancer in horror and disbelief. "Rendor!" she exclaimed. It had been six years since she had last seen him—or any reanimated corpses and skeletons, for that matter—and she would happily have gone another six, if not longer. The previous encounter—during which an undead former bandit had attempted to throttle her—had not been a happy one. *Rendor is a dangerous magician,* she remembered Valdira telling her, *and we would be unwise to underestimate him.* Fighting down the urge to panic, she threw a fireball, but Rendor extinguished it with a languid flick of his wrist before it detonated. Meanwhile, the skeletons, in particular, were drawing close. If only she had been able to memorize that wizarding spell that broke a necromancer's control over his creations!

Fortunately, Valdira—whose wide-ranging magical knowledge extended well beyond the limits of sorcery and wizardry—had taught Sinta two powerful necromantic spells, one of which she now used. "DISARTICULATE!" she shouted in the mystical language of the necromancers.

Never before having had occasion to use this spell in the field, however, she underestimated just how much *korethi* (or *pselikhost,* as the necromancers called it) she would have to expend to affect all sixteen skeletons. As a result, only the closest twelve collapsed into heaps of dry bones.

Even so, it was an achievement that visibly astonished Rendor, who was unaccustomed to magicians outside his esoteric specialty being privy to its secrets. His look of perplexity intensified when the spell he threw to incapacitate Othir failed to produce the desired effect, the latter's magic talisman having blocked it. Nevertheless, the four remaining skeletons were almost upon Othir, and the reanimated corpses would soon reach Sinta. Rendor had equipped some of the skeletons with improvised weapons. As a result, one of the survivors of Sinta's spell had a stray pickaxe handle, another a shovel. The undead corpses were carrying iron manacles for the sorceress's wrists and ankles.

Sinta was trying desperately to remember the other necromantic spell Valdira had taught her—one that canceled the key enchantment involved in reanimating corpses—but that had been four years ago. She had never needed it until now, and the correct combination of tongue-twisting necromantic syllables escaped her. Therefore she swung her quarterstaff instead, as hard as she could, at the closest attacker, dealing it a blow to the head that smashed in its skull and would have killed any living person. The reanimated corpse, which appeared to have belonged to a middle-aged townsman, had difficulty maintaining its balance for a moment, but then returned to the attack, joined by the other three. Despite sustaining further punishing blows from the quarterstaff, they quickly succeeded in overpowering the petite sorceress, after which they manacled her and stuffed a dirty rag in her mouth.

Othir was in no position to help, for he was beset by the four skeletons and soon also by the raven, which hoped to feast upon his eyes. He managed to knock the two unarmed skeletons to pieces, but the one with the pickaxe handle proved surprisingly adept at using it to deflect Othir's blows, while the one with the shovel had a long and dangerous reach. For its part, the raven made a determined assault on his face with its cruel beak. Othir had just managed to break the bird's back using the pommel of his sword, when the skeleton with the shovel succeeded in getting behind him and landed a heavy blow to the back of his head, just below his cervelliere, knocking him unconscious.

⚜

"My instructions are to kill you slowly and painfully," Rendor told Sinta, who lay sprawled upon the altar, as he—rather intrusively—searched her person, "and to do so with as much depraved sadism as I can muster, but you should know that I'm not necessarily committed to honoring the particulars of those instructions. Even though you stole my lizard—oh, and my knife, too, I see—I don't bear you any personal animus. Well, not much, anyway. My chief interest is that the news of your death should cause dear Valdira pain, so it doesn't matter to me if some of the gruesome details aren't strictly accurate. Tell me all about this enchanted coin purse of yours, and this magic amulet, and about any magical items your gallant but ineffectual would-be protector over there may have, and I would be willing to simply cut your throat. It would be over in seconds."

Despite her wide-eyed terror, Sinta remained clear-headed. As she saw it, her only hope was that Othir would soon regain consciousness and kill Rendor, but before he did, she needed to rid the room of the remaining undead for him. She therefore focused on casting her remembering spell (one of the few in her repertoire that required neither speech nor gesture), so as to bring to mind the necromantic word she had forgotten.

"So, what will it be?" asked Rendor. "Nod if you're ready to tell me what I want to know. Shake your head if you're opting instead for a grisly death through torture."

Sinta nodded emphatically, and Rendor extracted the rag from her mouth. "DE-VIVIFY!" she gasped in the necromantic tongue, and the four reanimated corpses reclaimed their rightful status in death.

Rendor stuffed the rag back into her mouth. "I'm not sure what you hoped to accomplish by doing that," he remarked. "They had already served their purpose." He looked at her with his bleak blue eyes. "Still, pointless as it was, your act of willfulness warrants punishment." He cast a spell, and Sinta felt as though her feet had caught fire. She screamed into the dirty rag, as the pain and fear sapped her *korethi*.

Rendor shook his head. "Let's try this again. Wouldn't you prefer a quick death?" Sinta nodded, but when he removed the rag, she cried, "DISARTICULATE!" Thanks to Rendor's having overlooked her enchanted hairpin, she still had enough *korethi* to cast the spell. She listened with satisfaction to the clattering of bones, the thud of the pick-axe handle, and the clang of the shovel, as the two remaining skeletons fell to pieces.

"You do seem to have rather odd priorities," remarked Rendor, gagging her anew with the rag, "but that is, of course, your prerogative." He cast another spell, this one causing her to feel as though her teeth were being filed down. "Just let me know when you've had enough!"

Othir drifted back to consciousness shortly before Sinta destroyed the skeletons, but he remained motionless on the ground for the moment, as he waited for his senses to resume their normal functions and start gathering reliable information about what exactly was going on around him. The situation was not good, he concluded, what with Sinta being tortured in chains on the altar, but at least Rendor was facing away from him. Getting to his feet in a suit of mail and covering the distance needed to attack the necromancer from behind without being detected would be a challenge, but he did not see what choice he had other than to try, and he could hope that his new ring would endow him with the necessary stealth to pull it off.

He waited until Rendor was busy taking the rag out of Sinta's mouth again. Seeing Othir get up out of the corner of her eye, Sinta did what she could to help him by using the last of her *korethi* to throw a heat spell on her persecutor, who swore horribly and stuffed the rag back into her mouth. The spell proved an excellent distraction, however, causing its target such discomfort that he had some trouble dispelling it, and Othir actually got within five feet of him before Rendor realized what was afoot. The necromancer then snatched up the magic knife he had reclaimed from Sinta, spun around, and managed to land a slashing attack to Othir's shoulder, though the knight's armor deflected the blade. The same could not be said for Rendor's black leather doublet, however, when Othir's sword struck it, entering the necromancer's body just below the sternum and causing irreparable internal damage. With all the force he could muster, Othir then yanked the weapon upward, causing a great deal more. He pulled the blood-drenched blade free, and Rendor collapsed, dead, onto the floor.

At this point, having failed to rest quietly until he had fully recovered from the shovel blow to his head, Othir became dizzy and hastily sat down on the floor himself. He remained there for several minutes, before getting back up to free Sinta from her manacles. While she waited, the sorceress managed to spit out the rag on her own. Her nerves were frayed from the magical torture, and her arms and legs were trembling, but the knowledge that Rendor was dead went a long way toward restoring her emotional equilibrium.

They both gave themselves awhile to recover before searching Rendor's body. When they did, they found a coin purse containing 1 gold *troog,* 6 silver *poog,* and 13 copper *tesh,* along with 7 gold ducats from the Grand Duchy of Modir. Othir volunteered that a Modiric ducat was worth roughly the same as a Hrissic pendragon, possibly a little more. They also found a sharp sheath knife, a rolled-up length of linen bandage, a moonstone, a dead mouse (a treat, presumably, for the raven), a length of string, a brass thimble, a crust of dry bread, and three glass marbles. Only the moonstone would prove to be magical. Sinta was correct in predicting that it afforded night vision, though unlike Othir's ring, it had no stealth component. She took the moonstone and the brass thimble and let Othir have the purse. She theorized that the glass marbles were physical components needed for some necromantic spell or other, but that was just a guess. In the end, she took them, too. Othir took the knife and the rolled-up bandage.

They searched the adjacent rooms but found no evidence that Rendor had been living in the catacombs. Othir suggested that they go to the neighboring village to see if he had been lodging at the inn there instead.

Sinta agreed. "He said he was acting on instructions. I want to know whose—and why."

Finding the innkeeper to be extremely cagey, Sinta opted for bribery. "Rendor is dead," she told him, producing a silver *poog* seemingly from thin air, "and so is his raven. They can't hurt you, no matter how many of his secrets you reveal." Pocketing the coin, the innkeeper admitted that the "dark magician" had been a guest at the inn, sleeping during the day and spending his nights at the necropolis. Another *poog* gained Sinta and Othir access to his room and to the stable.

On his horse they found a second enchanted moonstone, which Sinta claimed for Tamirandalia, and a potion, labeled in the necromantic tongue, that she pocketed for herself. Their search of Rendor's room was even more productive, yielding not only his traveling necromantic spell book, but also a brief journal in Ondiric and a small bundle of incriminating correspondence with Rendor's fellow conspirator, a sorcerer named Hrintenor, court magician to the Grand Duke of Modir. In addition to outlining the plot, these documents revealed Hrintenor's grievance as Grulfar's uncle. To her acute embarrassment and even greater disappointment, Sinta learned that the manuscript she had purchased from the peddler was a forgery designed to ensnare her. Togrod's library was a fabrication.

"The plot certainly seems to have been unnecessarily elaborate," commented Othir.

"Yes, but I think that reflects the personalities of both men," Sinta replied. "They clearly delighted in dreaming up ways to make it so. And in fairness to them, it came within an inch of succeeding."

Othir lay back on Rendor's unmade bed, for his head still ached from the shovel blow it had sustained. "The question," he pointed out, "now that you know who was behind the plot, is what are you going to do about it?"

17

Shindesh is a major port and naval base, notable chiefly for its large red-light district, where vice of any and all description is on offer. Visitors are warned that various venereal diseases run rampant there (see "Medical Facilities," below).

— *Esdiron on 12 Crowns a Day*

Sinta's personal preference at this point would have been to find a dark hole to crawl into, but she knew this was not a realistic option. Hrintenor was hardly likely to accept the failure of his revenge plot with equanimity, and as a sorcerer, he would know how to find her. Othir argued that they could not wait quietly for him to make another attempt on her life. Rather, the only choice was to go on the offensive. Sinta now had highly incriminating evidence in her possession, proving his culpability in a heinous plot against her. She should take it to his patron, Grand Duke Tanif, and demand justice. The grand duke was, in Othir's view, one of Ondiran's "less worthless" rulers, so it was conceivable he would give her a fair hearing.

All the same, Sinta found the idea of going to the grand duke alarming. The trauma of being tortured had only reinforced her tendency toward timidity, at least for the time being. In the end, though, she had to admit that Othir was right. Waiting for Hrintenor to dream up some nightmarish new plot was not an option. The evidence against him *was* damning. The grand duke might choose to ignore it, but she had to go to him and make her case.

⚜

Examining Rendor's journal and Hrintenor's letters, and then debating what to do about them, took until late afternoon. Sinta therefore paid the innkeeper for rooms for the night, along with a hearty supper to make up for their having skipped lunch. Although both she and Othir were worn out from the day's exertions and retired early, Sinta had a hard time falling asleep. Her mind dwelled on the traumatic events of the morning, though she also reflected on the fact that—unlike traditional methods—magical tortures did not usually leave physical wounds. Her nerves were frazzled, but at least she was not still hurting and at risk of infection. Once she did fall asleep, her familiar, upsetting dream returned. This time the tawny wolf was also gone, leaving just the gray one, which seemed even more thoroughly out of sorts than usual. She did her best to ignore the angry animal, as it growled and snarled and padded restlessly about, but in the morning she awoke still tired, her *korethi* only partially restored.

⚜

After breakfast, they saddled the horses, rode back to Feldross, and booked passage on a riverboat downstream to Shindesh, Esdiron's largest seaport. After two days on the river, they were obliged to wait two more days until the tides and winds were right for an Esdiric merchant vessel to sail for Modir and points east.

In the interim they explored the city. Sinta was eager to distract herself from the memory of her recent ordeal, the prospect of another ocean voyage, and especially the uncertainty shrouding her task at the other end of it. Fortunately, Shindesh was a bustling place with much to see—and, for that matter, to buy. Othir persuaded Sinta that she should upgrade her wardrobe prior to appearing before the grand duke. There was no time to commission a new dress, and *prêt à porter* would not be a fashion option for several more centuries, but she was able to purchase a hat similar to the one she had been thwarted from buying in Feldross, as well as a beautifully embroidered cloak that Othir had to admit rendered her significantly more stylish. His own attire was already the latest word in understated elegance, which did not prevent him from laying out quite a sum in silver *poog* for two new cloaks in rich fabrics not readily available in most of Ondiran.

While they were considering where to have lunch, Sinta and Othir stumbled upon a bit of guerilla street theater that drew their attention, especially once they realized it featured characters known to them. As they arrived, an aggressive flirtation was underway between a man in shabby aristocratic garb and a woman (actually a teenaged boy) in a preposterous burlesque of a noblewoman's gown, a flamboyant wig, and vivid makeup. Evidently the players were not striving for subtlety. The alleged nobleman was fondling some of the "lady's" more intimate body parts, when a youngster dressed as a pageboy burst on the scene.

"His lordship Legroshen of Grook, Count of Denchog, is returned from the hunt!" he proclaimed.

An actor, who bore a passable resemblance to the odious aristocrat Sinta and Othir had met on the road to Feldross, entered from what would have been stage left had there been a stage, wearing his own travesty of noble garb. "I am come," he drawled, in an exaggerated but recognizable impression of the count.

"Oh, my darling husband!" screeched the "countess," reluctantly removing her hands from her paramour's person, though he was slower to relinquish his grip upon hers. "And what did you bag today, milord?"

"Six boar, eight roebuck, and four peasants," he declared proudly. "Oh, and one cow, but that was by accident. And you, milady?

"I gave myself to three footmen and a stable boy," she replied at the top of her lungs. "And I was 'bout to favor the baron here, when you returned."

"Yes, quite right, most commendable," brayed the "count."

The audience, which evidently had a broad taste in satire, was laughing raucously, and there was a smattering of applause at this last line. Sinta wondered if her imperfect knowledge of Esdiric was obscuring some of the finer points of dialog, but Othir assured her there were none for her to miss.

Two "soldiers" with wooden swords dragged a small boy into view. "This beggar's brat stole a handful of rotten wheat," one of them announced.

"Off with his head!" screamed the "countess," waving her arms wildly.

"Yes, quite right. I concur," decreed the "count." "But be sure to flog 'im first!"

At this juncture the troupe's lookouts whistled loudly, warning that the city watch was approaching. The "baron" (in what Sinta had to admit was a nice bit of magic) threw a pellet to the ground, and the entire cast vanished in a dense cloud of swirling purple smoke.

The watchmen arrived shortly thereafter. Deprived of their intended prey, they seized members of the audience instead and beat them with wooden truncheons, until a disapproving Sinta murmured a brief incantation and gestured discreetly with her fingers, inducing such protracted fits of violent sneezing among the watchmen that their victims—as well as the rest of the crowd, including Sinta herself and Othir—were able to slip away.

18

Fin Whale. Known to our fisher folk as *tirot* or *tiret,* this whale is an extremely large fish that sailors recognize as a potential hazard to navigation. It has no teeth, but rather a series of hard bristles descending from its upper jaw. It spouts water in the air in a prodigious manner. Though the Tseren hunt it for its oil and blubber, it is too fast a swimmer to be an easy kill.

—*Aquatic Beasts and Monsters of the Sea, with True Descriptions and Illustrations from Life*

Given Esdiron's punitive customs regime, smuggling was a way of life for the sea-going population. The owners of the ship on which Sinta and Othir would be sailing therefore employed a young wizard—a teenaged Ondir with short black hair and mistrustful eyes—whose entire job it was to cast befuddling spells upon the customs officials who boarded the vessels in their fleet. As a result, the ship was cleared to sail without paying a single *tesh* in duty, notwithstanding its hold full of fine wine and fresh fruit. Sinta and Othir also escaped having to pay, for which they were particularly grateful, since the king had—in an effort to discourage the export of precious metals—recently decreed a special ten percent duty on all coinage leaving the country. As it turned out, there was just enough time, before the ship cast off and the wizard had to disembark, for Sinta to learn his befuddling spell in exchange for a wizarding spell she knew that prevented food from spoiling in warm weather.

⸙

The ship—named the *Desgrenokh* (storm petrel)—was another oaken cog, somewhat larger than the one with which Sinta had sailed from Tenefir to Mindor during the summer, but also somewhat older and a bit battered. The captain was a lanky Esdir, who seemed young for the job, though he had a firm grip on his crew, which comprised mostly fellow Esdir, but included an Inirochian first mate with a limp and a western helmsman covered from head to foot in geometrical tattoos. The captain was pleased to have a sorceress on board and agreed to a substantial rebate of her fare should he require her services during the voyage.

Under good conditions, two days would suffice to reach Modir, and the weather was in fact fine, with a brisk favorable wind. After about six hours of uneventful sailing, there was a whistling sound off the starboard bow and the boy in the crow's nest called down that a whale had surfaced there. Sinta and Othir, who had been watching the coastline go by from the port side, made their way unsteadily across the deck. The creature was significantly larger than the whales Sinta had seen that summer. At least seventy feet long and sleekly built, with a small dorsal fin two-thirds of the way down its back, it was swimming about fifty feet away on a parallel course with the cog.

"Keep an eye on that thing!" shouted the captain to his crew. "It could smash this ship to kindling if it wanted to!"

Remembering what the Tseren captain had told her, Sinta cast the mammalian variant of her animal charm. *We are your friends,* she told the whale. *Swim alongside and keep us company. Slap your tail if you understand me.* When the whale obeyed, Sinta approached the captain and told him not to worry. The animal now answered to her, and she would in turn answer for its good behavior.

She spent the next two hours asking the whale simple yes-or-no questions about itself and its life in the sea. "This creature is fascinating," she told Othir, who had been watching her commune silently with the beast, as it slapped its tail, or not, in response to her queries (or performed a barrel roll, if it did not understand them). "By far the most intelligent animal I've ever charmed. She's a mature adult female who's given birth several times and nursed each of the offspring until they were ready to survive on their own. She dives deep to catch fish—and apparently other things down there—but comes to the surface to breathe air. I asked her if she could communicate with other whales, and she indicated that she can. Evidently through sound. There aren't any of them nearby right now, but she can hear some that are far away. She also heard the ship's keel creaking. That's why she surfaced. I think she's as curious about us, as I am about her, so I've tried to tell her a few things about life on land, as well as ask questions, but I'm not sure that I've always managed to communicate in a way she could understand. Her world is so different from ours that I think her mind must be, too. Certainly her conception of time is. I have no idea how old she might be, and I can't think of any way to find out, except to ask whether she considers herself young or old, which doesn't tell us much."

Othir nodded, charmed by her enthusiasm for conversing with such an alien intelligence.

"Ships astern," called the boy in the crow's nest. "Two fast-moving craft!"

Sinta and Othir joined the captain on the stern deck. Both ships were smaller and faster than the cog.

"Pirates?" asked Sinta.

"Pirates!" confirmed the captain. "Unusual to encounter them this close to shore, but I suppose they figure that with those ships they can outrun any coastal patrols." He gave Sinta an urgent look. "Anything you can do, now's the time to do it."

Sinta approached the starboard taffrail. "Noble whale," she cried (for it always paid to put on a show for the client), "those two ships astern mean us harm. Protect us from them!"

After taking a fresh breath through her twin blowholes, the whale arched her long back and dived, disappearing from view. A remarkably short time later, the streamlined creature surfaced abruptly beneath one of the pirate ships, capsizing it and flinging everyone above deck into the sea (while causing injuries to those below). Although the ship then lazily righted itself, the yard had struck the water with sufficient force to snap crucial bits of rigging and partially collapse the sail. Meanwhile the whale dived again, so as to attack the second ship.

Perhaps her violent contact with the first had been unpleasant, for the whale now adopted a more conservative approach, hurling herself almost entirely out of the water, so that her massive body crashed back into the sea right next to the ship, causing a huge splash that nearly capsized it and pitched several terrified pirates overboard. A second breach was more successful, temporarily disabling the ship and throwing most of the remaining crew into the water.

"Excellent!" shouted Sinta. "Your work is done."

The whale dived, but soon protruded her head vertically just astern of the cog. Encrusted with barnacles, her skin was dark on the back and sides, but light underneath. With her relatively tiny—but actually quite large—right eye, she contemplated Sinta, Othir, and the captain, her pupil contracting, as it adjusted to the sunlight.

"Thank you," said Sinta. *You are free to go on your way, or you may come with us further, so we can continue our conversation. I leave it up to you.*

The whale slid back down into the water and presently resumed her previous position to starboard, where she expelled a prodigious plume of moist, whistling air and spent another hour listening to Sinta tell her about terrestrial life and occasionally answering additional questions about the sea.

Duly impressed, the captain reimbursed Sinta and Othir's fares in their entirety. "You're always welcome on my ship," he told them, as they disembarked at Modir. "Good bye and good fortune!"

19

Grand Duchy of Modir. Established during the Time of Troubles, Modir has been ruled by the House of Trentis ever since. Located on the southern coast, it is surrounded by the Duchy of Hriss on three sides. Notwithstanding its modest dimensions, the grand duchy is an important center for commerce, and successive grand dukes have earned reputations as liberal patrons of art and culture.

—*The Great Ondiric Compendium of All Knowledge*

The cog reached Modir early in the evening, time enough for Sinta and Othir to find rooms at an inn of acceptable quality. The low-lying city—sheltered behind a series of levies and causeways to minimize flooding from the powerful tides occasioned by the world's two moons—was dominated by the grand duke's palatial castle, which occupied the highest ground. And it was there that Sinta and Othir headed the next morning. To be sure, wandering into a grand-ducal castle from off the street and demanding to speak with the proprietor is not a guaranteed method of obtaining an audience, and it took most of the morning and any number of charm spells before the travelers were admitted to the throne room.

Grand Duke Tanif proved to be a young man, tall and well-built, with a thoughtful expression. The dowager grand duchess, who sat on a throne of her own to the right and slightly behind him, was a formidable creature, still handsome in late middle age, but with the fierce mien of a woman who knows where the bodies are buried for the simple reason that she oversaw the obsequies. Two dozen assorted courtiers and guards were also present.

"The sorceress Sinta, common subject of the Prince of Sildoor and daughter of the late apothecary Talman," the usher announced disapprovingly. "And her man-at-arms, Sir Othir, son of Osendir of Crin."

Though nervous, Sinta executed one of her best curtsies, thanks in part to a boost in confidence provided by the elegance of her new cloak. Othir bowed low with his usual grace and the assurance of years of training.

"What is your business before us, sorceress?" demanded Tanif.

Sinta swallowed hard and summoned up her best impression of her mentor, Valdira, who she knew would not be in the least intimidated by a mere grand duke. "I am here, your Serene Highness, to lay grave charges against your court sorcerer, Lord Hrintenor, who conspired with the late necromancer Rendor, son of Scrog, to bring about my painful death and reanimation into undeath, contrary to the laws of man and the precepts of virtually any religion one might care to name. I offer unimpeachable proofs in the form of incriminating documents—some in his own hand—concerning the planning of this vile scheme. I also offer sworn testimony from my own lips and those of the good Sir Othir, concerning the plan's recent execution and near success in the dismal catacombs of Chilchenteros, near Feldross in the Kingdom of Esdiron."

A scandalized murmur arose from the assembled courtiers. Tanif frowned. "These are indeed grave charges. Consorting with a necromancer is by itself a foul crime." He looked to the dowager, who nodded grimly. "But Lord Hrintenor has been our loyal servant, and our father's before us, for lo, these many years, and we are loath to believe him guilty of such base criminality. He must be present to hear and answer these terrible accusations against him." (Sinta bowed her head to concede this point.) "Summon his lordship at once," he commanded the usher.

While they waited, Sinta turned Hrintenor's letters, Rendor's journal, and the forged palimpsest over to the grand duke's castellan, who examined them with interest. Othir, displaying his usual nonchalance, chatted with a good-looking halberdier, one of several whose job it was to kill him, should he try to assassinate the grand duke or otherwise foment disorder.

Hrintenor soon swept theatrically into the throne room in his flowing black robe. Forewarned of the circumstances by the usher, he affected not to see Sinta and Othir. "Highness, wherefore am I summoned from my mystical pursuits in this peremptory manner?"

The grand duke gestured for him to sit. During the pause, heavy wooden chairs upholstered in red leather had been placed on either side of the chamber to accommodate the parties to the dispute. "You are here to answer the very serious charges laid by this young sorceress, who claims you conspired to murder her, and worse!"

Hrintenor turned to Sinta, his face displaying every sign of astonishment. "I have never seen this, this *person* before in my life," he declared.

"Nor I, him," retorted Sinta, "but not all crimes arise out of personal acquaintance."

Tanif held up a hand to betoken his desire for silence. "I take it, Lord Hrintenor, that you deny her allegations?"

"I do, indeed, your Serene Highness, whatever their particulars, as yet unspecified."

The grand duke turned to Sinta. "Very well, then. Sorceress, present your case."

This Sinta proceeded to do. With the benefit of an orderly mind, she made an orderly presentation, explaining the nature of Hrintenor's unfair grievance, his propagation of slanderous rumors, his solicitation of Rendor's aid, the hatching of their plot, the forging and sale of the manuscript with the help of the "peddler" (a minor wizard named Frogir), and finally the harrowing events at the necropolis. She referred repeatedly to passages from the documentary evidence, which the castellan laid out before his master on a low table. She elicited Othir's account of their encounter with Rendor and especially their discovery together of the documents implicating Hrintenor. "It is for your Serene Highness to decide," she concluded at last, "what punishment befits his lordship's amply demonstrated crimes. I crave no man's death, but I do desire justice—that and the freedom to live without the looming fear that this vindictive, spiteful magician will try again to avenge his depraved criminal nephew."

The grand duke stroked his chin thoughtfully. "We congratulate you, sorceress, on an effective presentation. Indeed, if you are as skilled in your spellcraft as you are in your advocacy—well, that remains to be seen." Sinta sat down, and he turned to Hrintenor. "What say you, court sorcerer, in the face of these damning proofs?"

Hrintenor stood, stroking his beard to mirror his master. "Indeed, Highness, 'twas a pretty tale, told by a pretty girl. But that is all it was—a tale, a tissue of vicious lies told by a madwoman in her cold fury, signifying nothing!"

"She did not sound mad to me," objected the dowager.

"No, your most Serene (and sagacious) Highness, she did not, for she has not the raving madness of the hysteric, but rather the calm, calculating madness of an ill-advisedly overeducated woman. Who but such a madwoman could dream up so bizarre and convoluted a plot against herself? That is not the mark of a rational masculine mind." He paused and directed his address back to the grand duke. "But let me begin at the beginning, Highness. I said that I had never seen this woman before, which was true. But now that I have heard her, I know her to be the same false accuser who brought about the shameful public execution of my dear nephew, Grulfar of Tiff. It would appear that she has conceived some insane grudge against our family, causing her now to come after me, as well—though perhaps she merely entertains the hope of supplanting me in your Serene Highness's service." He shook his head tragically. "Alas, such desperate schemes for the advancement of young magicians are not unheard of."

"But what of these documents," demanded the grand duke. "How do you account for them? Are these letters not written in your hand? They certainly appear to be."

Hrintenor shook his head. "Forgeries, Highness. I am ashamed to say that the art of sorcery includes spells for producing the most exquisite of fakes—which these most certainly are."

"And this knight of the realm? You accuse him of perjury?"

"I do, Highness. It is my understanding that he was expelled from the service of Lord Pirendor of Sirigot on account of his unnatural proclivities, which he deceitfully concealed throughout his training."

Sinta leapt to her feet. "Whatever his alleged 'proclivities,' Sir Othir is an honorable knight, who has served me loyally and well, and who has told the truth here today!"

"Aye," sneered Hrintenor, "loyal to the madwoman whom he serves—not out of sacred duty to the foreordained social order, but for gold. There is no reason your Serene Highness should believe a word out of this mercenary's tainted mouth."

Roused to anger, Othir stood. "Your Serene Highness, if this old mage were a young knight, I would slay him where he stands for these vile calumnies. Yes, I serve the sorceress Sinta for pay (as his lordship no doubt serves you), but I remain a knight of the realm, and I swear to you, on my honor, that I have told nothing but the truth in this matter."

The grand duke again raised a hand for silence. "Lord Hrintenor, have you anything further to say in your defense?"

The sorcerer nodded. "Indeed, I do, Highness. These persons put forward this purported correspondence of mine, but where is the other half? I freely give the castellan and his men leave to search my quarters for corroborating letters from the no doubt fictitious necromancer Rendor. They will find none."

"All that proves, your Serene Highness," retorted Sinta, "is that his lordship, like any prudent criminal, is sufficiently cautious in his villainy to destroy the evidence incriminating him."

"Enough!" The grand duke raised both hands this time. "Each side has argued eloquently and well. If this were a dispute between knights, tradition would call for a trial by combat. We see no reason to resolve a dispute between sorcerers any differently. We therefore rule that tomorrow morning, when the sun has cleared the Eastern Gate, Lord Hrintenor and the sorceress Sinta shall face one another on the greensward of the castle's lower courtyard to settle this issue once and for all. So we command, and so let it be done!"

20

Every practitioner brings to sorcery an innate magical power *(korethi),* but just how much varies widely from person to person. The key to successful sorcery, developed unceasingly over a lifetime, is the ever more efficient exploitation of this resource, so that any given spell will require less of it to be cast successfully. In this way an experienced sorcerer with less innate ability may well best an inexperienced one of greater natural talent.

— *The Mysteries of Sorcery Explained: A Layman's Guide, with Six Charts and Three Diagrams*

Dawn came cold and gray. Sinta awoke early and arose anxious, knowing the danger she would face—for a court sorcerer of many years' standing would be no trivial opponent. She had spent the evening with Othir, running through the spells she either knew, had with her, or could use her remembering spell to recall. Together they considered what Hrintenor was likely to throw at her, what protections he was likely to have, and what tactics employed against him might succeed or fail. Othir suggested Sinta's knowledge of wizarding spells might offer an advantage she could exploit, as Hrintenor was less likely to be familiar with those. He also loaned her Choss's talisman for extra protection alongside Grulfar's amulet. Nevertheless, Sinta would be facing Hrintenor alone, and she had good cause to be afraid. When the hour grew late, she therefore cast a spell placing herself into a deep trance to calm her troubled mind. When it wore off, several hours later, she drifted naturally into sleep.

⚜

One of the dowager's middle-aged ladies-in-waiting brought Sinta breakfast. "Her Serene Highness believes you," she whispered, "and hopes this ring will help you prevail." She held out an unornamented gold band. "It will protect your mind from magicks that seek to control, influence, or deceive you."

Sinta took the ring with gratitude and ate the breakfast likewise, though in the end she was far too nervous to keep it down.

At the appointed hour (the overcast that obscured the sun's clearing of the Eastern Gate notwithstanding), a contingent of guards took Sinta to the castle's lower courtyard. Another took Othir to join the spectators on a terrace overlooking it. A third brought Hrintenor. The courtyard was some twelve yards by twenty, and the guards positioned the two magicians ten yards apart on a lawn of short-cropped grass.

Sinta did her best to fight down the physical manifestations of fear she was feeling, but the pounding of her heart and the sensation of a fist gripping her insides refused to lessen. She shifted her weight anxiously from one foot to the other, and envied the seeming calm of her seasoned adversary. She was not pleased (though hardly surprised) to see that he carried a wand, which would concentrate and focus his *korethi* in much the same way as her enchanted hairpin concentrated and focused hers. *Your first priority,* she recalled Valdira instructing her, *when facing an opponent with a wand, is to take it away from him.*

"The contest shall begin upon our command and not before," declared Tanif from the viewing terrace, "and it is limited to the confines of the lower courtyard. If at any time one of you chooses to surrender, he or she shall be deemed to admit the charges made by the other against them, and will thus be legally liable. In this connection, we must point out that the punishment for bringing a false accusation is the same as for the crime of which the victim is falsely accused. Either of you is thus facing a potential sentence of death, subject only to a possible grant of clemency, whether by the other party or by ourselves." He raised one hand. "Very well, we declare the contest BEGUN!"

Sinta threw a quick disarming spell, hoping to take Hrintenor's wand, but she was not surprised to see it fail. She had already surmised that the court sorcerer was the most likely source of his nephew's amulet, in which case he would surely have equipped himself with similar protection. For his part, Hrintenor used the wand to cast some unknown spell against her, and she felt the amulet become warm against her skin, as it absorbed the *korethi* he had committed to it. Othir's talisman remained cool to the touch. As a wizarding ward, it no doubt worked on some other principle.

Sinta had a backup plan, however, for relieving her opponent of his wand. A summoning spell, cast on the wand rather than on Hrintenor himself, stood a good chance of success, providing he did not grip the device too tightly. She was relieved to see that he favored a light touch, holding the wand with the tips of his fingers like the bow of a stringed instrument, rather than clutching it in his fist like a weapon. She cast the spell just in time to disrupt the one he was casting back at her, and the wand did in fact slip through his fingers and fly across the courtyard toward her. She followed up immediately with three small fireballs in quick succession, forcing Hrintenor to choose between rescuing his wand and bathing in flame. He opted to dispel the fireballs, by which time the wand was safely in Sinta's hands.

There was a smattering of applause from the terrace, and Othir cheered.

Discomfited and embarrassed, Hrintenor gave an angry cry and cast a spell that caused the grass under Sinta's feet to grow uncontrollably, forcing her to dispel the enchantment or become hopelessly entangled. This distraction enabled Hrintenor to seize the initiative and pummel her amulet and talisman with two more spells, pushing them closer to the limits of their capacity.

The battle thereby entered a phase that was grueling for the combatants, but not very exciting to watch, as the two threw spell after spell with no visible effect, in a race to bring down the other's magical defenses by brute force before their own collapsed. Sinta felt her amulet heat up as it absorbed Hrintenor's spell power. It soon became painful, but with her adrenalin flowing, she was able to ignore the discomfort.

Eventually they each sought to mix things up a bit by casting spells designed to harm one another without being directed specifically *at* one another. Hrintenor thus cast an unusual spell that conjured up a cloud of jagged chunks of iron, which then fell like hail upon Sinta's position. She was able—but only just—to throw an invisible shield over her head, deflecting the descending shrapnel like a steel umbrella, but one piece nonetheless took a crazy bounce off a stone upon hitting the ground and gouged the bridge of her left foot, which was protruding out from under her dress.

"First blood!" shouted one of the spectators enthusiastically.

Sinta winced, but refused to let the pain distract her from throwing an obscure but effective wizarding variant of the fireball spell that immediately divided itself into six separate fiery projectiles that spread out and sought their target from different angles. Hrintenor managed to dispel five of them in time, but his aging reflexes were not quick enough for the sixth, which exploded upon hitting him. The blast was about a foot in diameter, prompting him to howl with pain, as it seared the flesh of his right leg.

"A palpable hit!" shouted Othir from the terrace.

The spell also succeeded in setting Hrintenor's robe on fire, and he lost valuable time and *korethi* extinguishing it. Another six mini-fireballs at this point might well have finished him off, but Sinta lacked the killer instinct to deploy them. Instead, she threw another spell intended simply to sap his defenses, whereupon he threw back a spell of his own. She felt Grulfar's overheated amulet shatter, overwhelmed by the power of it.

Sinta was tiring, and she had no way of knowing how strong Hrintenor's remaining defenses might be. At the same time, she knew the same must be true of him, while the burn to his leg and the pain it must be causing him had to be sapping his spell power significantly.

Indeed, looking for a way to conserve his strength, Hrintenor created the illusion of a blast of frost, which required far less *korethi* for him to produce than a real one, but just as much of an opponent's *korethi* to dispel. The dowager's ring, however, left Sinta undeceived, enabling her simply to ignore the phantom frost. The audience gasped as it appeared to envelop her—without doing the slightest harm. Having spared herself the time and effort of dispelling the illusion, Sinta could now punch back hard with a "magician's fist." To her surprise, she succeeded in knocking the old man to the ground. His magical defenses were down.

Sinta now executed one of the potential endgames she had mooted with Othir the night before. First she cast the befuddling spell she had learned in Shindesh, leaving Hrintenor momentarily confused and disoriented. That gave her time to cast a complex memory spell, permanently wiping from his consciousness all knowledge of the mystical language of sorcery—and thus of all the spells he had ever learned—effectively returning him to the level of a beginning apprentice. A third spell similarly expunged from his memory all knowledge of his grudge against her. And finally, with the very last of her *korethi,* she put him into a deep sleep, to make clear to the audience that the contest had ended and she was the victor.

Afterward, the guards carried Hrintenor off in chains to the castle's dungeon, while Othir bandaged the wound on Sinta's foot. Descending to the courtyard, the grand duke offered his congratulations and invited Sinta and Othir to a festive lunch.

"Richly though he deserves it, please do not put Hrintenor to death," Sinta entreated, during the meal, as she gratefully accepted a second helping of pheasant. "He is now both old and powerless. Let him retire to the countryside and raise geese, cultivate vegetable marrows, or engage in some other harmless pursuit."

Tanif stroked his chin thoughtfully. "This quality of mercy does you credit," he said. "It makes me regret even more that I cannot offer you the post of court magician in his stead. Alas, the job has long been promised to my cousin Ferin." He smiled ruefully. "Never attain a position of power," he advised, "if you also have aunts. They will thrust their offspring upon you—and will not be denied!"

"The grand duke is a man of wisdom," opined Othir to Sinta, once they were alone again. "Aunts are a scourge and a menace to the powerful and powerless alike. Let us hope that Hrintenor has some still living—and yet more who may come back to haunt him from beyond the grave!"

Sinta, who had no aunts, was not prepared to believe the species so uniformly malign. She sought to change the subject. "I'm afraid your talisman did not survive the battle," she said, returning it to him, cracked in half. "It must have been overpowered by the same spell that shattered Grulfar's amulet." She sighed. "Hrintenor came a lot closer to winning than it appeared, so I'm lucky to have escaped with my life."

Othir turned the broken talisman over in his hand. "The grand duke's herald was making book among the spectators. You were a long shot at six-to-one. I wagered all seven of Rendor's gold ducats on you—so, I'd say your luck was also mine!"

Despite her depleted *korethi,* Sinta slept soundly that night, undisturbed by dreams of wolves of any description, and she woke the next morning feeling fully refreshed.

21

Several spells have been devised to locate lost or missing objects or creatures. They are not considered difficult, but their chances of success correlate closely to the amount of spell power the sorcerer is prepared to commit to them.

— *The Mysteries of Sorcery Explained: A Layman's Guide, with Six Charts and Three Diagrams*

Sinta and Othir remained for several pleasant days in Modir as Tanif's guests. Due in no small part to Sinta's skill as an apothecary, the wound on her foot declined to become infected, and it had begun to heal nicely by the time they left. Their subsequent journey home, while not without incident, involved no dangerous encounters, whether with trolls or pirates or anyone else. They had been gone rather longer than their fellow residents of the apothecary's shop expected, but no one was tactless enough to express disappointment at their return. To the contrary, Pentigor—who arguably would have had the most to gain from Sinta's having gone missing—was pleased once again to have someone with whom he could talk at immoderate length about new herbal remedies or the latest refinement to traditional methods of distilling alcoholic tinctures.

Othir spent some time familiarizing himself with Talindor and its opportunities to spend some of his newly acquired treasure, while the horses felt relief to be home and free from the prospect of further encounters with ships and the sea, at least for the time being. Sinta resumed the task of setting up shop as a sorceress for hire. She commissioned a small sign to hang next to the one depicting a mortar and pestle that advertised the apothecary's. It featured the character from the sorcerers' syllabary traditionally used to symbolize sorcery. Few would know what it meant, but it looked suitably occult. In smaller letters below, the sign stated in Ondiric, "Freelance sorcery at reasonable rates."

Five days later, Sinta's first client climbed up the stairs to her study. A scruffy fourteen-year-old boy, dressed as a tradesman's apprentice, he gave her a skeptical look. "They say you're a sorceress—that you know how to do magic."

Sinta acknowledged the accuracy of these reports, so far as they went.

The boy produced a handful of mostly tin coins from his pocket. "Somebody's taken my dog, Gorth. Do you think you can find him?"

Sinta nodded. "I have successfully recovered lost dogs in the past," she admitted. "What does Gorth look like, and when did you last see him?"

Don't miss

Tales from Ondiran, Book Three,

Sinta
Sorceress-Detective

by Sedigitus Swift

Turn the page for a preview!

Excerpt from *Sinta, Sorceress-Detective*

Unfazed by the thick clouds blocking the light of the two moons, the lone figure in a hooded cloak moved with preternatural assurance through the darkness, while ascending the rugged western slope of the high hill. Upon reaching the castle at the top, the figure—in a remarkable display of free climbing that would have dismayed the structure's long-dead architects—exploited the shallow angle formed by the meeting of the curtain wall with a massive round tower to scale thirty feet of sheer stone in less than five minutes. Finding no guards atop this section of the battlements, the intruder quickly crossed to the other side and began a more challenging ascent of fourteen feet on a curving diagonal to a window on the eastern side of the tower. Although now in full view of much of the castle, the climber remained undetected—due in part to the cloudy night, but in part also to the chameleon-like qualities of the hooded cloak, which provided an effective magical camouflage against the mottled gray stone. Several tense minutes passed, as the intruder clung precariously to the side of the tower, while contriving to open the latched window without breaking it—or falling some forty feet to a bone-shattering death on the cobbles below.

Once inside, the hooded figure dropped lightly onto the wooden floorboards of the large workshop or laboratory that took up the entire eastern half of this level of the tower. The room was overflowing with esoteric objects and mysterious equipment, ranging from an enormous armillary sphere near the window to a fully articulated walrus skeleton with thirty-inch tusks by the door. Paying these interesting distractions no heed, the intruder instead maneuvered sure-footedly through the cluttered darkness to a ladder leading to an open trapdoor in the ceiling. Climbing it in something approaching silence proved difficult, but with time and care the intruder emerged successfully into a small but similarly crowded bedchamber.

It was a warm night, and the room's half-naked occupant had kicked off his bedclothes. In his mid-thirties, he was unexceptional in appearance. His slow, steady breathing confirmed that he was still asleep. The intruder approached and studied him dispassionately for a moment before drawing a long, narrow-bladed dagger and thrusting it with both force and precision between the fourth and fifth ribs, through the musculature of the intercostal space and the fibrous tissues of the pericardium, and into not only the left but also the right ventricle. A swift jerk freed the enchanted blade, while slicing open the punctured heart. Blood gushed from the wound, as the sleeper gasped and opened his eyes, awake and uncomprehending in the dark for just seconds before he succumbed to unconsciousness. Less than a minute later, he was dead.

With an indistinct vocalization, the killer dipped a finger in the blood and placed a single daub on the victim's forehead, before cleaning the dagger, returning it to its sheath, and making for the bedchamber window. There the clouds chanced to part for a moment, and the light of the larger of the two moons flooded in, illuminating for the first time the distinctive face concealed by the hooded cloak—angular, high-cheekboned, and female.

Evidently the cloak had more than one magical quality, for after taking hold of special handgrips sewn into the fabric and placing her feet in a pair of cloth stirrups, she leapt from the already open window, stretched out all four limbs, and glided forth like a flying squirrel. Banking sharply around the tower, she cleared the battlements of the curtain wall and swooped down the side of the hill to the bottom, thus effecting her escape.

About the Author

Sedigitus Swift is a historian by day and a pseudonymous fantasy author by night (as well as during eclipses or otherwise under cover of darkness). When not diverting himself by writing offbeat medieval fantasy novellas, he specializes in the perplexities of modern Central and Eastern Europe. No doubt he has other equally perverse interests, but we are not currently certain exactly what those might be.

If you have enjoyed this book, you might consider subscribing to his engaging monthly newsletter, *The News from Ondiran,* at www.sedigitus.com, for advance word on upcoming works, insights into the creative process, and choice bits of Ondiric lore. It's free!

And if you're feeling really benevolent, you might leave favorable online reviews anywhere such reviews congregate. They don't have to be long or detailed, but they will help other readers find this book.

www.sedigitus.com

www.ingramcontent.com/pod-product-compliance
Lightning Source LLC
Chambersburg PA
CBHW030022060826
49398CB00031B/184

* 9 7 8 1 9 6 1 8 5 2 0 3 7 *